WINGS TO FLY

WINGS TO FLY

•

Beate Boeker

AVALON BOOKS
NEW YORK

Published by Thomas Bouregy & Co., Inc.
160 Madison Avenue, New York, NY 10016

Library of Congress Cataloging-in-Publication Data

Boeker, Beate.
　　Wings to fly / Beate Boeker.
　　　　p.　cm.
　　ISBN 978-0-8034-9902-7 (acid-free paper)
　　1. Life change events—Fiction.　2. Seattle (Wash.)—Fiction.
I. Title.

PR9110.9.B64W56　　2008
823'.914—dc22

　　　　　　　　　　　　　　　　　　　　　　2008005924

PRINTED IN THE UNITED STATES OF AMERICA
ON ACID-FREE PAPER
BY HADDON CRAFTSMEN, BLOOMSBURG, PENNSYLVANIA

Chapter One

She saw it a split second too late. A blur of green and beige—where had it jumped from?—loomed up at her left without warning, threatening like a monster out of a nightmare. The high screeching of tires shrilled in her ears, on and on and on and on, until it felt as if it came from within her. And then, just as her brain finally reacted to the emergency and her foot hit the brake in an desperate attempt to stop, she felt the impact.

It took her car from the side, lifted it up and tossed it away as if it were a ball in the hands of a child. Cathy was thrown to the side like a used rag.

She cowered down by instinct and gripped the steering wheel as hard as she could. A film in slow motion, she saw the world sliding by. The dusty tarmac of the street, twisting like a snake, a birch tree so close she could make out the white bark and dark-green leaves on the lower branches before it galloped past her; and then, a long brick wall, zooming in until the rest of the world was blotted out by brick and mortar. The bricks were red. Faded orange red, brown red, dried-blood red.

This is NOT happening! The thought flashed through her mind, even when she knew she had no chance.

The car stopped half an inch from the wall.

Cathy sat and stared. Orange red, brown red, blood-red. A large piece of mortar had fallen off at one corner of the wall.

She looked down. The knuckles of her hands on the steering wheel were white. One fingernail stuck in the plastic surface and broke off when she eased her hold. She didn't feel anything. And then the thought that had dominated her for hours came back, useless now, like a hen without head, but still running. *I can't be late.*

The door at her side was wrenched open.

"Are you hurt?"

Startled, Cathy looked up, straight into a frowning face. She saw him thrown in sharp relief, with every detail stamped into her brain as if she had never seen a face before. He had brown eyes. With yellow flecks in them. Like a lion. Curious.

"Are you hurt?" he repeated and touched her shoulder.

She opened her mouth to answer his question, but what she really said surprised herself. "I don't have time."

He blinked. "Excuse me?"

She swallowed and struggled out of her seat, but her knees shook so hard, she almost lost her balance.

He gripped her by the arm. "You're not okay." He searched her face with narrowed eyes.

Cathy took a deep breath. For some reason, it sounded like a sob. She had no time to cry now. She had to get to the interview in time, if it was the last thing she did. Afterward, she might look back and take stock. Not now.

He bent down to her and forced her to meet his eyes. Though she was standing now, he still towered over her. His sun-bleached hair flopped forward into his face. Beneath his suntan, he was pale, and there was a mixture of fury and concern in those lion eyes. "Are you hurt?" he repeated, emphasizing every word.

She shook her head, feeling nothing. It was as if she was standing next to herself, watching herself and commenting on everything, while her real self was numb.

"Are you sure?"

He had a compelling voice. Like whiskey. Yes, if whiskey could speak, it would have such a voice. She'd always loved the golden brown color and peaty smell that took her immediately to windswept hills and wide blue skies. She gave a start. He had asked her something. "I'm okay." Her voice sounded rough.

Step-by-step, things started to feel more real. Screwing her eyes together against the blinding sun—her sunglasses must have fallen off—she tried to take in the situation.

The monster was a van. It was parked at the other side of the road. Beige with dark green letters that said MICK VANDENHOLT. The sun glistened on its clean windows, which reflected the light. It did not seem to have suffered much damage, if you didn't count a dent at the front and some scratches in the paint. Well, it was a giant compared to her little yellow Honda Civic.

The heat rising from the street crept up her legs and made her panty hose stick to her legs.

Cathy stared down the street. Thank God she had turned onto a smaller side street, off Mercer, just a minute before the accident, in her effort to get a better orientation by following the silhouette of the Space Needle.

She whirled back to retrace the route of the accident. Her small Honda faced back in the direction where she had come from, having spun around after the impact. It stood halfway on the sidewalk, as if she had parked at a rakish angle. Cathy swung around and discovered a stop sign that left no room for doubt—she had overlooked it, maybe because it didn't show well against the facade of the Starbucks just behind it, but probably more because she'd been so busy deciphering street names and searching for them in her map. It was no wonder the accident had happened.

It was a wonder she had survived. But she had no time to be grateful now. She had to go.

Now.

Struggling down the panic that rose within her, she took a step closer to check her car.

He had watched her getting her bearings without comment, but as he followed her look he said, "I'm afraid it won't take you anywhere anymore. At least not today."

Something cold gripped Cathy's heart. Then she saw

it too. The van had driven into the side of the Honda, crushing the metal of the fender straight into the tire. The black rubber material wobbled around the rim, good for nothing.

The victim of her hectic driving said something.

Cathy jumped. "Excuse me?" Her voice sounded like a foreign thing.

His lion eyes seemed to assess her. "Should I take you to the hospital?" He hesitated. "I believe you're in shock."

She shook her head, impatient. "Oh no. I'm all right, really." At least her knees were almost steady now, and she wasn't two people anymore.

Realizing she had been less than gracious, she tried a smile. "Thank you. I'm very sorry."

When he smiled back, a dimple deepened in his left cheek. It transformed his lean face and gave him a charm she found irresistible. "Are you sure you don't want to go in for a checkup? I could drive you there; it would not be a problem."

Maybe it was his smile; maybe it was because she was still rattled. She heard herself say, "Can you drive me to the Convention Center?"

He opened his mouth and closed it again. The distant honk of a ferry vibrated as a deep bass through the noise of the traffic. A wave of stifling air enveloped Cathy. It smelled of hot tar.

"To the . . ." He seemed stunned.

"Do you know where it is?" Cathy said. "The Washington State Convention and Trade Center." She was so desperate to get the job, she could not allow herself to be distracted by something as unimportant as a close escape from death.

His eyes never left her face. "Why, yes, but . . ."

"I have a job interview at four." Sweat burst out on her arms and her face as she realized she might miss her chance.

He glanced at his watch. "It's a quarter to."

Cathy felt hot tears welling up in her eyes. The disappointment hit her like a physical blow, straight into her stomach. After all she had done. The weeks of secrecy and preparation. Reading every imaginable book on how to sail through a job interview. The dreams about setting up her own, independent life. The dreams about Seattle. . . . It all flashed through her mind, like a jigsaw someone had torn apart. Unable to say a word, she swallowed, but the lump in her throat only grew bigger.

"We could make it," she suddenly heard him say. "It's just a few blocks away."

"Really? Oh, could you please drive me there? It's important!"

His eyes grew intent, assessing her. Cathy met his gaze without flinching, squinting against the sun. Her heart hammered against her chest. This was her only chance. If he said yes, she might reach her goal. She balled her hands into fists, willing him to agree.

Finally, he nodded. "Why not? Get in."

Cathy felt herself go limp with relief. She dove back into her car, retrieved her handbag from beneath the seat, and ran to his van. Her back had barely connected with the seat when he started the engine and shifted into gear. It was cool inside and smelled of wet earth.

"I have to call the police and report the accident." He sounded as if he did this kind of thing every day.

"Sure." She'd agree to anything. Anything. Nothing was worse than having to return to Spokane empty-handed, to have failed yet another time at trying to do something all on her own.

"I guess they'll call the repair service to get your car off the road."

"Fine." She had one eye on the clock. Ten to four.

He threw her a look as if he wanted to check that she was capable of taking in what was happening.

For a time, neither said anything. The engine hummed through the tense silence as he navigated across a street and they went down at a steep angle toward Elliott Bay. Cathy caught a glimpse of sparkling blue water before it disappeared behind the glass front of a skyscraper.

In silence, they drove on. Then he pointed upward. "Do you see that gray building over there, with the glass front? That's the convention center."

"It's built across the street!" Cathy couldn't believe her eyes.

"Yeah. We Seattlelites firmly believe in building things in several layers. We even have a park, built right across I-5. It's a bit farther on." Mick's voice held a mixture of irony and affection. He flicked on the turn signal. It clicked with a metallic sound through the silence. Cathy tapped her foot. Just around the corner, and she'd be there. Five to four. She moved to the edge of the seat and put her hand on the door handle.

"How do I know you'll come back?" The question sprang at her like a tiger.

Cathy froze.

Of course. She'd been stupid to think he would trust her, with two damaged cars, the police, and the insurance companies to deal with. She cast him a haunted glance, not knowing what to say.

"What am I going to tell the police?" His voice sounded calm. "I don't even know your name."

The car stopped close to the curb. Cathy glanced at the large glass doors that led inside the convention center, promising her a new start, if only she could get there. She checked her wristwatch. Three minutes to four.

Without allowing herself to think, Cathy grabbed her purse and threw it into his lap. "There you are. Driver's license. Credit card."

She jumped out of the car and ran for the entrance.

Whirling though the revolving doors, she slithered to a stop at a large desk with the sign INFORMATION hung above it.

The woman seated behind it looked up, her mouth forming a big *O* by Cathy's sudden appearance. However, she did not say anything, just raised her impeccable eyebrows with faint disdain.

Cathy's skin crawled with a thin sheen of sweat. She refused to think of the way her hair would look. Like a bird's nest or something. Summing up all her confidence, she said, "Hi. I'm Catherine Albray. I've got an interview with Leslie Peters at four." She suppressed her breath, which came in little gasps.

The cool woman gave her the once-over, then resumed typing on her keyboard without uttering a single word. Cathy clenched her teeth. She hadn't made it just in time in order to be delayed by some arrogant secretary. Smoothing back a tendril that had escaped her thick coil of hair, she raised her voice. "I have an appointment with Leslie Peters at four."

The woman typed away without looking up. Her fingernails were a glossy pink, ten perfect matches. Cathy did not want to start a fight in a place where she had to leave a good impression, but the pressure and anxiety of the last hours seemed to take on a life of their own and burst like bubbles inside her. "Are you here just for decoration?" She narrowed her eyes. "If yes, let me know, and I'll hang my coat on you and go find somebody who knows how to speak."

The glossy woman threw her a bored look and murmured without moving her lips, "Leslie is not in the office."

Cathy was bereft of speech. She pivoted around, fighting to hide the tears smarting in her eyes. Could there have been a misunderstanding somewhere? Had she made a mistake with the time or the date? She opened her bag and hunted through it for the magical piece of paper that had promised her a new life.

She had just found it when the revolving door spit out another visitor who hurried straight up to her. The newcomer stopped in front of Cathy and offered her hand, "Hi. You must be Catherine Albray. I'm Leslie Peters. Sorry I'm late, but I'm sure Donna here told you I would be back in a flash."

Cathy hastily blinked away the tears and peered into Leslie's shrewd brown eyes.

Leslie turned to Donna and held out her hand. "Just in case we don't see each other anymore, I'd like to wish you all the best for your new start."

Cathy stared at the two women shaking hands. Donna's smile was no more than a stretching of her lips. So that was it. Donna had taken the liberty to be in a bad mood on her last day.

Pushing her thoughts away, she tried to compose herself. *Be cool. Like a cucumber.* She followed Leslie through the sunlit hall to an elevator that smelled of metal, dust, and the perfume of the woman who must have used it last.

The fragrance slammed her back to her tenth birthday. Her aunt used the same perfume. What was the name again? Yes, Cascade. She had always used it, from the first day they had come to live with her. Cathy had been so bewildered, had struggled to come to grips with the total upheaval of her world. Her aunt and uncle had made every effort, she could see that now, but at the time, all she wanted was to return to England, to turn back time, to make it all un-happen. It was early in the morning, and they were all gathered around her birthday table, gifts piled high, threatening to glide off. Gifts she didn't want. And when her aunt smiled at her and said, "Why don't you start to unpack?" she burst into tears. It was Dan who gathered her into his arms and comforted her. It was Dan who told them that at home, they always made a circle and danced around, singing all the birthday songs they knew before they started to open the gifts. But by then it was too late. It hit Cathy for the first time. Her parents were dead. She broke down completely, and if it hadn't been for Dan, she would never have made it.

"Did you have a good trip?" Leslie startled Cathy back into the present.

"Oh yes, thank you," Cathy avoided her eyes.

"It's sometimes hard to find a parking place . . ." Leslie continued as they got out of the elevator, ". . . particularly when it's the last day of a show like today. Did you have trouble finding one?"

Cathy just managed to suppress a hysterical giggle. *Oh, no, I left it smashed on the curb. Very neat, it takes up little space.* Pulling herself together, she answered, "I . . . I left it just a few blocks away."

They passed a woman in sneakers and dusty slacks. Her hair had become undone and she had black rings beneath her eyes. With dragging steps, she schlepped a black bag, a cardboard box, and a folding chair. Cathy looked at her and instantly knew how she felt. The last day of a show . . . pandemonium on the exhibition floor, workmen roaring around with fork lifts, carrying wooden crates in a multitude of sizes. Every spot covered with cardboard boxes, folding tables, trash, wrapping material, impromptu picnic sites and people, people, people milling around like ants. Cathy could almost feel her feet hurting again, could feel exhaustion washing over her. Doing a trade show took you to the limit. Every time.

They reached a white painted door that stood halfway open and allowed a glimpse of a small office. Leslie pushed the door open and entered. "Oh, John, you're already here." Turning to Cathy, she said, "This is John Marks, our Human Resources manager."

Cathy shook his hand. For once, a man was at her eye level. She took a deep breath and told herself to relax. This was it. Now she had to prove what she had learned.

It was cool in the office, with a faint smell of menthol. In spite of that, Cathy felt sticky and surreptitiously wiped her hands on her skirt after being seated.

She forced herself to breathe evenly. What was it the textbooks had recommended? She should be calm. In control. Sure of herself and her value. *What value?* She wished she were far away. If she failed now, she would never dare lift her head again. She would continue to live at Dan's side forever and ever, and he would tell her what to do at every single turn of the way. She shook herself. *This is not going to happen.* She turned to Leslie.

Leslie bent forward and opened the battle. "I know we've already talked a lot on the phone, but why don't you tell John a bit about yourself, and why you would like to work here?"

Cathy crossed her legs and leaned back in her chair, focusing on John. Now was her chance to change it all. She felt like a runner at the Olympic games, just after the gunshot that started the race. With a voice rough from nerves, she said, "When I graduated from high school, I already knew I liked to work with people and to help them along if they were stuck somewhere. I find the whole service industry fascinating."

She sounded like the textbook. Dry and boring. Learned by heart. Which it was. She balled her hand into a fist, her fingernails digging into her skin. Without pausing for breath, she rushed on, "So I decided to study business and economics, figuring it would offer plenty of opportunities." *At least, that's what Dan had said.*

John nodded, his rimless glassed blinking in the light.

"Would you mind starting a little bit earlier? I notice you have a British accent."

Cathy flushed. She hated to talk about her childhood, but she forced herself to smile. "Yes, I can't hide that, can I? I grew up in England until I was nine, then we came to stay in Spokane. And this is where I've lived ever since." Why did she sound so stilted? She'd practiced talking about it for so long, in front of the mirror in her bedroom. It shouldn't hurt anymore.

John's face didn't reveal what he was thinking. "I see. From what you said about yourself, I think being a sales representative should fit the bill nicely. Have you considered that?"

A sales representative? Oh, no! That had not been part of the job description! She was nowhere persuasive enough to be a rep. Hunting for a polite refusal, she hid her fear in clasped hands. "I thought about it, but I don't want to travel all the time."

Then she caught herself. Darn. This was going to lead to exactly the topic she had wanted to avoid. And here it came. "But you're willing to move to Seattle, leaving your family and friends behind?" John asked.

Cathy gritted her teeth. "Oh yes. A onetime move is totally different from being constantly on the road." She hoped they would swallow that. No need to tell them the truth, to tell them she was scared to death, to tell them it was the most daring thing she'd ever done.

Leslie had listened without once taking her eyes off her and now asked, "But I seem to remember you have friends in Seattle, don't you?"

Why did the image of the lion-eyed man appear before her inner eye? "No." Cathy shook her head. "But I'm confident I would settle quickly." *Perhaps. Probably not.* She'd never been on her own before. Ever.

Leslie nodded. Cathy's mouth was dry. She plunged ahead, eager to get over this hot topic. "After my studies, I found a job with the company Christie Cards in the marketing and sales department. They print greeting cards with unusual designs. Part of my job involves trade fairs."

Cathy drew a deep breath. *Show them you know the business,* she reminded herself. "I am responsible for organizing all the documents, prototypes, sales material, the booth as such, invitations to customers—well, all the preparatory stuff—then attending the show, selling the collection, and afterward, dismantling everything and clearing it all up. In the end, I compile the statistical figures to see if the whole thing was worthwhile." She made a move with her hand. "The last day of the show is the most exhausting one." She smiled in a convincing way. At least she hoped it looked convincing. She had checked it out on the mirror, but if not done right, it sometimes ended up a little frayed at the edges. She bit her lip. *Dear God, let it soon be over.*

Leslie nodded and leaned over the table to get a bottle of water. She opened it and filled three glasses, pushing one over to Cathy. Then she asked, as if they were making small talk at a cocktail party, "You sound as if you love your job. Why do you wish to change?"

Cathy was prepared for this question; she'd constructed an answer in a sleepless night, wondering what would sound most credible. "Christie Cards is a small company and there is no way to get ahead. Organizing a show from the other side sounds like an interesting challenge."

This was perfectly true, even if it wasn't her driving motivation. But she couldn't very well say, "For private reasons." That sounded as if she'd had an affair with her boss, or was thrown out because nobody could stand her, when in fact, it all came down to having a dominating brother.

Glad she'd gotten the answer credibly off her tongue, she bent forward to pick up the glass of water—and froze. Her heart missed a beat. A black smudge disfigured her left stocking just at the side of her knee, with a ladder running all the way down to her shoe. Panic-stricken, she recrossed her legs the other way round, twining them around each other to hide the ladder as much as she could.

Her hands shook. She abandoned the project of taking the glass in spite of her thirst. Leslie and John had not noticed anything amiss. Leslie now explained the different shows Cathy would be responsible for. She kept on talking for several minutes, giving Cathy enough time to recover, but when John asked her a short time later if she had a best friend, she was rocked off her fragile poise again. She didn't have a close friend; she only had Dan. Nevertheless, she nodded. "Yes."

John scrutinized her as if her soul was visible on her face, and maybe it was, though she desperately hoped not, and said, "How would your best friend describe you? What would he or she say is your greatest strength and your greatest weakness?"

Cathy had expected these questions, but she'd never been asked to give them from somebody else's point of view. Rubbing her shoulder with concentration, she said. "I . . . uh . . . he . . . he would say I'm straightfor-ward, honest." What he'd actually said was, "You should stop walking around with your heart on your tongue," but she couldn't repeat that.

John did not bat an eyelid. It was impossible to guess what he was thinking.

He probably dissects people's souls before breakfast every day. Cathy was surprised by the bitterness that rushed through her.

John put his head to one side, his eyes never leaving her face. "And the negative one?"

Cathy swallowed. She had a cramp in the leg that was curled around the other. How was she ever going to get up again? "He'd say I'm stubborn."

Oh no. Not the right thing to say. No, definitely not. Strong-willed. Determined. That would have been much better. But the damage was done. She'd never had such a terrible interview before, and if it continued much longer, she was going to burst into tears. Besides, she wasn't stubborn. Not at all.

Somehow, the interview went on, but to Cathy it was all in a haze. Like a tournament—each question an obstacle, she had to approach it in a gallop, judge the size, jump, and, hopefully, get over it without breaking her neck. She wanted the job so much. It had become a symbol of all she wanted to achieve. Independence. Freedom to make her own decisions. But it felt as if it was slipping from her grasp, even as she was trying to hold it with all her might, fighting every inch of the way.

When Leslie said good-bye to her a long hour later, Cathy felt as if she had spent five years in the building. Her head throbbed and the muscles in her cheeks were stiff from smiling too hard. Scuttling sideways so Leslie would not discover the ladder on her leg, Cathy escaped through the revolving door. A giggle that was close to tears escaped her. Did it matter so much to have a torn panty hose at the most important interview of a lifetime? Wouldn't it have been better to admit to an accident and mention it in a joke? Leslie was probably going to entertain a whole group of friends tonight by describing the funny woman who had applied for a job, knotting her legs in incredible positions and moving like a crab. Besides being sweaty and red in the face.

Cathy tried to take a deep breath. She had to put this experience behind her. Maybe she'd tell her grandchildren about it one day, laughing. Maybe. Maybe not.

The air outside was still so hot, it felt as if a hair dryer was directed at her. Without thinking, Cathy opened her handbag to take out the keys for her car. Then it hit her, as if a curse had struck.

Of course. How could she have forgotten? She had given her purse to a total stranger. Who was probably buying a trip to Hawaii with her money right now. How could she have been so stupid? If Dan should get wind of it . . . She cringed. Who'd ever heard of giving your driving license and credit card to a total stranger? She'd been stark, raving mad. What on earth was she going to do now? She rubbed her left shoulder and frowned into the sun. She was stranded.

Chapter Two

Standing like a statue, she clutched her handbag like a lifeline. The air had a faint, salty smell that reminded her of vacations at the sea. Or did she imagine it? She would love to live here, surrounded by water. And she would love that job. If she got it, it would be worth a wrecked car—but maybe not the loss of all her savings and more. As it was, she may end up without the job and without any money. Darn.

Tapping her foot, she eyeballed the street. She hadn't even told him how long it would take. Maybe he'd been here and gone again, thinking she had stood him up. She stared across the street. Quite a few vans passed, but not the one she was looking for. Though she hardly remembered it anyway. Cream, was it? With some green writing. She'd forgotten the name. Careless. She'd forgotten to remember the license number too. Really, how stupid could one get?

With a frown, she remembered the day that was responsible for her standing now in the middle of Seattle in the heat. Mary-Lou, her colleague at work, had started the whole thing one wintry morning when she said with her voice rough from smoking, "You won't believe what I did last night!"

"You met the man of your dreams, but he wore white socks, so you jilted him." Cathy grinned across the desk at her and bent down to switch on her computer.

"I wish I had." Mary-Lou stood on her toes in front of the shelf to get a folder. "No. Much worse."

"You went to the cat zoo."

Mary-Lou stopped in her tracks and stared at her. "To the zoo? What zoo? Are you crazy? You'll only find me in a zoo when every single nightclub—no, make that every house—in Spokane has burned down."

Cathy held up her hands. "Sorry, sorry. But from the way you started, I thought it was something extraordinary." She took her cup of coffee and stirred it until the coffee almost swashed over the rim. "Come on, spill the beans, I'm dying of curiosity."

Mary-Lou returned to her desk and sat down, but she did not open the folder. Instead, she placed it in front of her, folded her hands with the bloodred fingernails on top, then leaned across it and said, "I taught my grandmother how to fill out a check."

Cathy stopped to stir and stared. "You did what?"

Mary-Lou nodded, satisfied with the effect of her

announcement. "Incredible, isn't it? Did I tell you my grandfather died two weeks ago? A true macho man, he was. But my Gram thought he was a kind of semi-God or something and never did anything without him. Now that he's gone, she has to do it all by herself, but she's swamped with the tiniest things."

Mary-Lou's telephone rang. "Oh, shoot! I thought I'd destroyed it yesterday when the receiver fell on the floor." She watched it with raised eyebrows, but when it didn't stop ringing, she sighed and finally answered it, never noticing that Cathy's mouth had dropped open. Because, in that instant, she could see herself, lost like that grandmother, if she should ever try to live without Dan. She'd never realized how dependent she was. It scared her to death.

A car honked and rushed by, startling Cathy. The glass door behind her swung open with a sound as soft as moving air, and the girl from the reception desk came out.

Dana. No, Donna, that was her name. Cathy tried to smile at her, but Donna did not deign to acknowledge it and ambled away in a swinging, sensual way Cathy would never achieve, even if she trained for hours. She had the longest legs Cathy had ever seen.

With a sigh, Cathy closed her eyes and leaned against the wall of the building. The gray concrete beneath her jacket still breathed the heat of the day.

All of a sudden, another horn rang out to her left. She swung around, and with relief that made her feel almost giddy, she saw the cream-colored van pulling up at the curb. The man with the lion eyes jumped out and ambled over. Mick Vandenholt. That was the name on the van. She watched him. He was wearing jeans and a white T-shirt and for some reason she could not make out, he appeared to be fresh and cool, suntanned as he was. Like some advertisement for healthy living. He was even taller than she remembered, and rather lean, not on the muscular side like Dan, who could intimidate you by just standing in a door like a rock, immovable, inflexible. Mick reminded her of a lion. Smooth movements, a force controlled, but in a relaxed way. There was something reassuring about him, but she couldn't pin down why he made her feel this way.

She hurried to meet him. "So you haven't decided to start a better life on my credit card." Her voice wobbled with sheer relief.

He returned her smile, and she saw the dimple reappear in his left cheek. "I was tempted. But it would have been hard to disguise myself as a five-foot woman."

They were standing next to the van now. "How was your interview?"

She couldn't say why it happened at this moment. Maybe it was the strain, finally snapping her nerves, now that it was over; maybe because she had failed; maybe the simple friendliness in his voice, as if they were longstanding friends. Whatever it was, it made her burst into tears. "I'm sorry." She sniffed. "I'm not usually so strung out."

She didn't dare look up into his face, but she heard him

opening the door of the van, then a tissue was put into her hand. "Why don't you sit down," he said.

Cathy climbed into the van, struggling to stop crying. But the more she tried, the more tears seemed to come. She hid her face in her hands, attempting to suppress her sobs. Why, oh why, did everything have to go wrong? Now she sat there, crying like a baby in front of a stranger who probably thought she was crazy enough to be carted off to the loony bin. The tears streamed through her fingers and dropped onto her skirt.

Something large was put into her lap. She took away one hand and peered at it. A Kleenex box. Gratefully, she took more tissues and blew her nose. With an effort, she tried to compose herself, but it was a long time later when the sobs abated and she was able to take a deep breath.

She didn't dare to lift her head. Her eyes would be red and swollen.

"Do you want to talk about it?" he asked.

She couldn't hear any curiosity in his voice, just a mix of hesitation and warmth.

All at once, she wanted to tell him. Not all of it, of course. No need to divulge that she was constantly under the influence of her brother and had no experience living on her own. But it would be a relief to share the final disaster. It would become more manageable, somehow.

"I applied for a job as an event coordinator." She cleared her throat. "I would have been responsible for five different shows. The annual gift show, the stationery show, and some others."

"The green show too?" Mick started the motor and glanced over his shoulder to check for other cars before he moved away from the curb.

She nodded. "Yes. Do you know it?"

"I sure do. My livelihood is based on gardens." He smiled to himself as if it were a source of great satisfaction.

So that's where his tan came from. "Well," Cathy rubbed her left shoulder. "Then you probably know all about it. Organizing the booths, getting the best exhibitors, calming nerves at the show, making sure everything runs without a hitch, and so on. The logistics, particularly, are a challenge at each and every show." She went on to explain loads of details that probably bored him. But she couldn't help herself, she had dreamed about this job for so long . . . and had kept it a secret, because otherwise, Dan would have talked her out of it. It was a relief to be able to share it. Even if it was over now.

While Mick's van crept through the clogged streets, she said, "Well, it's not going to be. At the interview, they turned me inside out, dived into my soul, found nothing noteworthy there, and just when I thought I might still make it, I discovered this huge hole in my stocking"—she pointed at it—"and I forgot anything impressionable I might ever have been able to say. It was horrible. You know, they're trained to see the things you want to hide."

Mick glanced at her knee. "It doesn't show very much. They might not have noticed."

Cathy sighed. "I don't know. But it cramped my style. And in general, I can be quite convincing."

He smiled. "I know."

He turned at a green light and accelerated down the steep road. A street sign flashed by. OLIVE WAY. What a poetical name. A second later, they crossed beneath the monorail. Cathy craned her neck to see it better. She'd read about the Seattle Monorail, but she'd never seen it before.

"But for somebody who only had one interview, you sound as if you already know quite a lot about the job. That should be very convincing," Mick said.

"I'd better know a lot about it." Her voice sounded bitter. "After all, I was an exhibitor at shows, so I've seen plenty about the other side of the business at least."

"Well, if you're a businesswoman, I wonder still more about it, Catherine Helen Albray." He waited for a car to pull out of a parking space, then slotted the van into the just-vacated space. Behind them, a car honked. Mick cut the engine and swung around to her, a frown on his face. "How come you trust a stranger so much you just hand over your ID and money?"

She stared at him. "It was an unusual situation! That job is—was—desperately important to me! And I had to give you something to make you believe I wasn't going to bolt, leaving you to pay the repair for the van."

His expression was rather forbidding. "And can you explain to me why you climb into my car and let me drive you away without even once asking where we're going?"

She swallowed. He was right. She was much too used to trusting, as if she was only eighteen. "I . . . I thought you were taking me to my car," she said with as much dignity as she could muster.

"I'm not."

Cathy felt as if someone had punched her straight into her stomach. Unable to move, she stared at him. What was he going to do? She'd often heard about murderers being the most charming people. But before she could gather her wits enough to jump out of the car and run for it, hiding in the throng of people on the street, she heard him say, "I'm taking you to the police."

She caught her breath. Her eyes widened. Had he told the police it was a hit-and-run accident? Were they going to charge her? Maybe even arrest her?

The hint of a smile crept into one corner of his mouth. "No, not what you're thinking. When they came to take official note of the accident, they wondered about your absence. I explained you had an important job interview and . . ." He hesitated, then grinned, ". . . they might have gotten the impression we've been friends since kindergarten."

Cathy couldn't help it, she giggled. "Do you think they wouldn't have swallowed the truth?"

"I wasn't going to try finding out," he said, his voice

sounding dry, "finding it still rather difficult to digest it myself." He looked at her for a second, but she couldn't even start to imagine what he was thinking. "By the way, your car is at the garage already, and I hope they'll call me tonight with more information."

Cathy felt a wave of heat mounting to her face. She should have asked about her car ages ago. "Thank you." She bit her lips. "How on earth did you manage that in such a short time?"

Mick grinned. She really liked his smile. "Henry is an old friend. We went to school together."

He checked his watch. "We'd better go. They want you to sign some statements, and I promised I'd take you down to the police station as soon as you had finished."

Their steps sounded hollow on the linoleum floor. It gleamed like a polished mirror and reminded Cathy of a hospital floor. The hall was bare, with slanted spots along the ceiling that highlighted the stark white walls in regular intervals. A faint smell of detergent wafted through the chilly air. It was as comfortable as a fridge.

At the far end of the hall, behind a wooden reception desk so small it seemed lost, sat a police officer with more hair than Cathy had ever seen. It grew out of his ears and nose and crowded down from the top of the head toward the eyes, as if in another year or so, it would cover every inch of his face. Light blue eyes peeped out from the jungle and twinkled when they saw her. "Ah, the runaway lady." His voice was a deep rumble.

Cathy froze and wanted to retreat a step, but Mick put his hand on her back and, with gentle pressure, propelled her forward.

The hairy officer wheeled his chair to the side with a swishing sound and fished some documents from a pile to his left. He hadn't noticed her reaction. "You were lucky it was the van of an old friend you hit on your way to the interview."

"Yes." Cathy met Mick's eyes. The smile that lurked in those golden brown eyes made her feel as if it were true, and she'd known him a long time already.

"Did the interview go okay?" the police man asked.

This question was not going to shake her a second time. She smiled. "It's always hard to tell what kind of an impression one leaves behind. They said they'd be in touch soon."

He nodded. "What kind of a job is it?"

All of a sudden, Cathy realized this was no casual small talk. She held her breath. The police suspected they had staged the whole thing to claim the repair from the insurance! The idea had never entered her mind, but when she shot a look at Mick, she discovered with a shock that he knew all right. There was a grim touch about his mouth she'd not seen before. She wondered if he had seen the implications before letting her go. If yes, he had taken a risk almost as big as she had.

Stunned by her realization, she took a second too long to answer. "It's with the Convention Center."

The light blue eyes stared unblinking at her, showing as much emotion as a pair of stones.

She drew herself up. "I had the interview with John Marks and Leslie Peters."

"John Marks?" The officer lifted his eyebrows. "Nice guy. I happen to know him. I'll see him tonight." He handed her several printed pages. "Please read these carefully and sign them at the bottom."

Cathy closed her eyes for an instant. So what if the police checked up on her only a few hours after she had entered a town for the first time in her life. She wouldn't get the job anyway.

She went with Mick to the side and checked the documents. Yes, it had been her fault. Yes, she had overlooked the stop sign. Her insurance company was not going to be pleased. Well, if they were going to be difficult, Dan could . . . No. Dan couldn't. She was going to make it herself. She was not a baby any longer. She signed the documents with a wobbling hand and handed them back.

When they left the police station, a telephone rang. Mick reached into his back pocket and pulled out his cell phone. "Henry, hi. . . ." He listened to a babbling voice. "Yes. . . . Okay. . . ." The babbling grew louder. Mick frowned. "That doesn't sound good. . . . Are you sure? . . . Hold on a sec, she's right beside me."

He turned to Cathy. "This is the repair service. Henry will manage to repair it all right, but not tonight. And tomorrow is a holiday. Will the day after tomorrow do?"

Cathy blinked. "But I . . ." Her voice trailed away. She had to work the day after tomorrow. And Dan . . . oh, Dan should get lost. With grim determination, she nodded. "Okay."

Mick's eyes seemed to assess her for a second, then he talked into the phone. "She says okay, Henry. Thanks for pushing it. Bye." He put the cell back into his pocket and eyed her. "You're good at making quick decisions, aren't you?"

Cathy blushed. It didn't sound like a compliment, somehow. She raised her chin. "Yes."

He smiled. "So what would you like us to do now?"

The traffic roared past and blasted a mixture of hot air and exhaust fumes at them. Cathy looked up at Mick. She'd only understood a minute ago how much he had done for her. Before her courage could fail her, she said, "I'd like to invite you out for dinner."

His eyebrows lifted.

Cathy hastened to add, "To . . . to say thank you for everything." And then, because he still didn't say anything. "Besides, I'm starving."

He laughed and took her by the arm. "Okay. Let's go."

When he led her past his van without stopping, she looked at him, a question in her eyes.

"I'll take you to Pike Place Market," he said. "It's just down the block. I won't tempt fate twice by giving up a perfect parking space." He glanced at her. "Have you heard of Pike Place?"

Cathy nodded. "Yes. It's a market for fresh stuff, particularly fish, isn't it?"

Mick nodded. "Yes. It's where we go to feel European." He glanced at his watch. "Though by now the real bustle will be over."

A short walk brought them to the corner of the low market building. The first thing Cathy saw was a huge African-American lady with a billowing dress in pink and lilac. She stood with closed eyes on the sidewalk and sang as if she were all alone in the world. Her voice was deep and resonant, her song slow and sad.

Cathy slipped, someone seemed to grab her foot, and she almost fell. Keeping her balance with difficulty, she discovered her heel had gotten stuck between two cobblestones and tried to ease it out again. Mick watched her with a mixture of a frown and a laugh on his face. "You'd better take my arm."

"Thanks."

Her hand seemed small on his arm. She could feel his muscles moving beneath her fingers. Her heartbeat accelerated. She glanced at him, and suddenly, she noted it again. He moved with the same grace as a lion, the same controlled strength. With smooth ease, he matched his steps to hers. Cathy smiled.

"The restaurant is right there," Mick pointed across the street at a low building, painted in pale green. Curlicued letters read *Da Gino* over the oblong windows. Next to the door, a wooden sign announced FRESH PASTA AND FINE CUISINE. The air-conditioning felt cool when they entered, but above all, a delicious smell envelopèd them. Cathy realized she had not eaten anything since breakfast. Her mouth watered. The small square tables were covered by red-and-white checkered cloths, with a candle on top of each, fixed in simple brass candleholders.

They were lucky and got a table right at the window. Cathy fell into the chair Mick pulled out for her. "What a day." She had started with so much expectation. *No.* She stopped that thought. She didn't want to think about her smashed-up dreams. She wanted to enjoy dinner. Time enough to cry later. She grinned at Mick. "I'm ravenous."

"Then you've come to the right place."

"Do you come here often?"

He pushed back his hair. "Not as often as I want to. It's a favorite place of my mother's. She sometimes invites us here on the weekend."

Cathy lifted her head. "Us?"

"Yeah. My sister, if she doesn't have to work, her friend, me, and any friends who happen to be in the vicinity. She's . . ."

At this instant, a small man bustled up to their table. His green pinafore stretched across his round midriff in a way that made Cathy wonder when the seams would crack.

"Buona sera, Mick." He beamed at Mick and twinkled at Cathy. "Buona sera, signorina." Cathy smiled back.

Mick said, "Hello, Gino. It's great to see you."

"It's been some time since we've seen you." Gino spoke with an accent that showed more in the rhythm of the words than in the pronunciation. It reminded Cathy of an Italian song she'd once heard on the radio.

Mick sighed. "Yes. But you know how it is with work."

Gino nodded. "Sì!" As he talked, his hands whirled over the table. He set their places, lit the candle, and placed a small basket with fresh bread as well as a round dish with olive oil and a few glossy olives onto the table. "It must be hot out in the gardens right now."

Mick laughed. "It sure is."

"How is la mamma?" Gino handed them the menus.

"She's fine."

Cathy stopped listening and watched them. Mick managed to seem absorbed in his discussion, yet his eyes met hers from time to time with a smile.

When they had accepted Gino's recommendations for the day, and he had rolled with all speed to the next table, Mick said, "I'm sorry. I forgot that Gino would want to have news of the whole family."

"It's not a problem. I like him. Have you lived in Seattle for a long time?"

"All my life."

"And do you like it?"

"Love it. Of course, you have to put up with traffic jams and the occasional drop of rain . . ." he grinned, ". . . but I love being close to the sea and the mountains at the same time. Besides, you can have everything. Bustling life in the center or solitude out in the woods. It depends on you."

Cathy took a deep breath. "Yes." Oh, how she wanted to move to Seattle.

Gino brought them a selection of grilled vegetables combined with small pieces of tomato and garlic tossed in olive oil as a starter.

Mick took his fork into his hand. "Enjoy your meal."

His lion eyes smiled at her, and all at once, the sounds of the restaurant receded and left only them. A warm feeling of contentment started to sing inside Cathy. She smiled back. "Enjoy yours. And thank you for bringing me here."

During the meal, they compared living in Seattle to living in Spokane, then they compared his pasta arrabbiata to her tortellinis with sage-spinach-Parmesan filling. Somehow, they meandered back to talking about Seattle, and from there, it was only a step to regale each other with stories about the places they had visited during vacations. In the end, they ended up laughing about summer-camp stories in the mountains until Cathy had to gasp for breath and wipe away some laughing tears. She remembered other dates when conversation had proved to be difficult before they had finished their appetizers. Not so with Mick. When she thought back later, she couldn't remember a single awkward moment.

The restaurant filled with people until they were surrounded by a humming crowd, faces smiling with the prospect of good food and a holiday before them. The clink of glasses and the smell of the dishes mingled in Cathy's mind. She felt happy and light, and it didn't matter anymore that the day had been less than perfect.

"Would you like some dessert?" Mick smiled at her.

Cathy hesitated. "I've had too much already but the tiramisu on display at the entrance looked wonderful."

His eyes twinkled. "Would you like to share one with me?"

"Yes!" He did feel like a long-standing friend. What was it about him that made her feel so much at ease? Was it because he was so effortlessly polite? So easy, so unpretentious? Maybe it was the way his brown eyes met hers. Serious, yet with a hidden smile somewhere in their depths. The yellow flecks were sometimes almost hidden, sometimes clear. She wondered what made them change.

When Gino had served one dish of tiramisu with two plates, Cathy pressed the spongy cake with the mocha flavor and the creamy topping to the top of her palate. Maybe life was still worthwhile as long as things like tiramisu existed.

"Do you know what tiramisu means?" She licked off her spoon.

"I didn't know it had any meaning," Mick said. "Is it Italian?"

"Yes. It means 'Pull me up'. Isn't that a fitting name?"

He laughed and leaned back in his chair. "Very. I feel . . ." He looked up, and all at once, he cut off what he had been about to say. His face froze, then his gaze dropped back to her face with an expression she could not describe.

It was gone in a moment. He seemed to want to say something, then stopped himself, and got up in slow motion while staring at a point behind her shoulder.

Cathy spun around. A slim woman of about forty approached the table with outstretched arms. She moved forward as if she were about to enfold Mick in her arms, then thought better of it and contented herself with beaming at him. "Mick! What a nice surprise! I haven't seen you in ages!"

Mick's smile was strained. "You've seen me last week, Frances."

"But that's what I'm saying!" She turned to Cathy.

Cathy jumped up and put on a polite smile, then caught her breath and stared like a child in front of a fairy princess. *There is a beauty that stops the wind in its tracks and makes the trees bow down with reverence.* She couldn't remember where she had read it, but the passage could have been composed for the woman in front of her. Frances' face was a perfect oval with delicate bone structure. Around it billowed a cloud of wavy brown hair, cut in an expensive style that gave her a windswept appearance without minimizing her elegance. Cathy swallowed.

Mick introduced them, standing as if he were frozen stiff. "This is Catherine Helen Albray."

Cathy pulled herself together and held out her hand. "Everybody calls me Cathy, though."

Mick seemed to have changed into a butler, he was so formal. "My mother, Frances Bernett. . . ."

Cathy blinked. His mother? She was much too young to be his mother! And why did he call her Frances? How odd.

Frances smiled at her, her brown eyes shining. There

was a likeness. Those were Mick's eyes. Without golden flecks, though. She was dressed in black slacks and a sporty white blouse, but she wore them with the natural elegance of a queen.

". . . and her husband, David Bernett."

Cathy tore her eyes away to face the man she had not noticed next to his stunning wife. But when she shook hands with him, she realized he may not jump to the eye, but would be a force to be reckoned with. He had the quiet manner of somebody used to being in control. His gray eyes seemed to assess her in a second.

"I'm sorry we're butting in," Mick's mother said. "But we saw you sitting in here when we walked by, and I simply had to run over and say hello."

"That's no problem at all." Cathy smiled. "We've just reached the coffee stage anyway."

Frances subsided into a chair with effortless elegance. "So we might join you?"

Cathy liked her and didn't mind at all, but out of the corner of her eye, saw that Mick still stood like a tree and had not uttered a sound. She turned to see his face better, a question in her eyes. Mick glanced at her, again with that curious expression she could not read, then dropped into his chair as if resigned.

David pulled out a chair, settled between Frances and Cathy, and crossed his legs, one ankle on his thigh. He had a certain patina that shows on rich people. Nothing so crude as a Rolex on his wrist, oh no. It was more a certain cut about his clothes, the subtle smell of his aftershave, the whiteness of his teeth. When Cathy met his eyes, she had the strange impression he was laughing at her. Then she realized it was a trick of his eyebrows. One was higher than the other, making him look skeptical, even if in repose.

Her eyes were drawn back to the beautiful woman beside him. Frances dazzled her with a smile that revealed a pearly row of even teeth. "I'm so glad that we finally get to know you, my dear," she said. "Mick has already told us so much about you. I've been wanting to meet you for ages."

Cathy blinked and opened her mouth.

At this moment, Gino appeared at her elbow. "Buona sera, bellissima; buona sera, David."

Cathy stopped listening and stared at Mick. He had a girlfriend? The warm feeling inside her disappeared as if someone had smacked her. He didn't meet her eyes but stared with a frown at his mother.

Gino poised his pen. "Are you sure you'd like nothing but coffee?"

"Yes, dear." France smiled.

"The usual?" Gino asked.

Frances nodded.

"Two black coffees, then." Gino addressed Cathy. "How about you, signorina?"

"I'll take a coffee with sugar and cream, please." Cathy felt as if she were part of a play. It seemed so unreal.

"Espresso for me." Mick sounded almost rude.

Cathy blinked. What on earth was happening?

Gino nodded, smiled at them all and hurried away.

Cathy drew a deep breath. But before she could tell Frances she had mistaken her for some other girl, Frances bent toward her and murmured with a twinkle in her eye, "You know, whenever I wanted to meet you, Mick said you had to work so hard at that dreadful job of yours that—"

Mick interrupted her. "Frances, it's not . . ."

"Oh, I'm sorry!" Frances lifted both hands. "I hope you're not offended." Her large eyes were dancing. "It's just that I never liked working, so I can't imagine anybody else doing so!"

Cathy had to laugh. "No, no, that's fine," she said. "But I'm not . . ."

Frances reached across the table and took her hand. ". . . You're not working tonight, but enjoying the evening with Mick, I know, so we won't butt in for long, don't worry. I know you don't have a lot of time for each other, since you live so very far away. Did you fly down today?"

Cathy was bewildered. "No, I came by car. But I really think you mistake . . ."

"Here's the coffee." Gino slid the cups onto the table. "And here's the espresso."

Cathy threw a wild glance at Mick. He had balled his fists. "Frances, I'm sorry, but Cathy . . ."

Frances let go of Cathy's hands and clasped his instead. She was shining with joy. "Oh, now I understand!" Her voice jubilated so loud that the guests at the table next to them turned around and stared. "Cathy is a surprise for my birthday party tomorrow! What a smashing idea, Mick! I'm so happy, even if I have now inadvertently 'opened' my gift too early!"

Cathy was dumbfounded.

Frances veered around to her husband, her shining hair swinging with the movement. "Isn't it sweet of Mick?"

David smiled at his wife. Her enthusiasm seemed to bounce off his calmness, but his voice was warm when he replied, "Yes, darling. It's a lovely idea."

Frances turned back to Cathy. "You can't imagine how much it means to me, my dear!" She tossed down her coffee and jumped up. "But now we'll leave you." She flung out her arms. "You don't have much time together, and I dare say you wish me to Jericho! We'll have plenty of time together tomorrow."

She bent forward and gazed into Cathy's eyes. "Will you come a little earlier, so we can talk? I'd love to get to know Mick's girl better."

Cathy was mesmerized. Feeling unable to disillusion her, she nodded. Frances probably wouldn't have registered any protest, either.

With a fragrant touch, she kissed Cathy on the cheek. Then she hugged her son, whispering audibly, "She's utterly lovely," into his ear and left, waving at them every few steps.

David stopped a second longer, looked at them both and said, in his calm way, "Thank you. It means a lot to her. She was very unhappy." Then he followed his wife.

Cathy stared at his retreating back, not quite sure if she understood what was going on.

Then she faced Mick. He avoided her eyes.

"Mick." Cathy cleared her throat. "How . . . ? What . . . ?"

Mick jumped up. "I've got to explain this to you." He threw a hunted look around the restaurant. "But not here."

Chapter Three

Gleaming white sailing yachts rocked in the calm water, highlighted by the evening sun. Farther out, the water stretched in a blue so deep it drew you out and made you forget all your land-bound worries. To the right, a row of bluish mountains seemed to hover above the horizon. Cathy tried to recall their name. Olympic Mountains? That might be right. Mick had driven north, straight from the center of Seattle in less than half an hour's time. A slight breeze relieved the heat of the evening and cooled the hot skin at the back of Cathy's neck. Mick saw her taking it all in and grinned. "It's quite a sight, isn't it?"

Cathy nodded, unable to find the words to describe her feelings.

"It's called the Shilshole Bay Marina," Mick said as he led her toward the pier. "I believe it's the largest marina in the Northwest, and of course my boat is the best moored here."

She threw him a glance. Bragging didn't seem to be his style. He didn't notice her reaction, but shaded his eyes with one hand and scanned the pier.

The jetty was built far out into the water, offering room for hundreds of gleaming sailboats and yachts. Late sun rays slanted across them and created long shadows in crooked forms. Cathy's shoes clattered on the hot concrete as they went to the far end of the jetty. Here, smaller boats were moored. Mick stopped in front of a wooden motorboat. It was painted in broad stripes of bright yellow and garish green and should have been ugly, but time had mellowed the effect. The chipping paint together with the less-than-average size even gave it a certain charm. Cathy couldn't suppress a smile. "Is this yours?"

Mick nodded and jumped on board. Then he turned and held out a hand to help her. "It's not exactly a status symbol, but it offers a quick getaway whenever I need a little distance. So it's quite precious."

His hand was firm and warm. Cathy misjudged the distance and ended up right in front of him, her nose almost touching his shirt. For a second, she could smell his skin before he released her and moved away. She took a deep breath.

He smiled at her with his lion eyes. "Is it okay if I take you out before I make my confession?"

Cathy nodded. She wasn't used to boats. Her knees wobbled.

As if he knew what she was thinking, he asked, "Or do you easily get seasick?"

She shook her head. "No."

Mick rummaged in his trouser pocket, took out a key and opened a box underneath a seat. "Why don't you sit down right here." He indicated a seat to the left of the motor. The motor was fixed at the back of the boat, dipping into the water at the outside. Taking out two yellow cushions, Mick gave one to her and put the other on his own seat at the other side of the motor.

With the ease of long practice, he arranged his long legs beneath the seat, then grinned at her. "There's going to be an infernal noise at first, but we'll soon be farther out and then we can just let her drift along."

Mick tore at the line. With a stutter, the motor became alive. A cloud of diesel smoke billowed up, and then they were moving. Mick steered the boat along the coast, going south, with one hand relaxed on the tiller.

Cathy leaned back and folded her hands in her lap. Her eyes devoured the rugged coastline. It seemed incredible that so close to this tightly packed city there should be so much nature, so many trees, such blue water. After some time, the land to her left ended in a pointed tip, which they passed in a wide berth.

And then, they faced downtown Seattle. As they put-putted closer, Cathy's eyes grew large. She'd seen pictures of the Seattle skyline, but being here, feeling it, breathing it, was so different, it made her light-headed.

With delight, she discovered one landmark after the

other. The Sky Needle, Seattle Center, the low building of Pike Place Market where they'd just been, the ferries, and behind her, the Cascade Mountains as a dramatic backdrop. She knew them all by heart, from the hours she had secretly dreamed over pictures of Seattle, hoping it would be her new home. Each name sent a thrill down her back, standing for freedom and independence. All at once, she had to laugh at herself. *It's just another city. It's up to you to make it.* But that didn't help. Her heart still beat quicker whenever anybody mentioned Seattle.

The gleaming surface of the water stretched out as a polished surface to her right, to her left, everywhere. Not a ripple showed. Along the coastline, the soft evening light was fading, but here, it was still shining, floating like a rosy-blue cloud above the perfect sheen. Straight ahead, Mount Rainier guarded the city from the sideline. Its craggy surface was softened by the lavender light; its round top nudged the fragile evening sky.

Cathy smiled. *What a friendly mountain, with just the shape a mountain should have.*

A dry voice within her corrected her, *It's a volcano.*

A sigh escaped Cathy. *Oh well. A beautiful volcano, then.*

Farther on, something white arched out of the surrounding buildings. The Seahawks stadium. On the pictures she had seen, taken from above, it looked like a giant clam, halfway opened to reveal the treasures within.

How intense were the feelings this building harbored. Shouted slogans—Go, Go, Go!—enthusiasm that built up like a wave until it broke foaming and terrible, utter despair with hidden tears, jubilant success making you jump sky-high. Cathy watched the sunlight settle on the white wings of the stadium. Though she had never been there herself, it still held a special memory. As if it had happened yesterday, she remembered the weekend her team had won the high school softball tournament. It had started so wrong. On the Friday before, she told Dan that neither her aunt nor her uncle were going to watch her game. She was shattered. Nobody was going to cheer her on, and it was such an important game. She had tried to suppress her tears, had forced herself not to think of her parents who would surely have shown more interest if they had been alive, but Dan knew her pretty well. And before she knew what was happening, he had sold his coveted ticket at the Seahawks stadium for the top game of the year and came with her instead to her little provincial tournament. She still had the picture showing them after the award ceremony. It hung above her bed. She, grinning with triumph from ear to ear, waving her blue and yellow flag, all arms and legs; Dan, with his arm around her shoulders, smiling down at her with pride, very grown-up and good-looking. Quite a few of her friends tried to get to know him better, but they never got far. They'd always had each other, and it had always been enough. Until now.

The motor sputtered as Mick accelerated. Cathy took

a deep breath. Feeling the gentle breeze on her arms, almost blinded by the golden light all around her, even the interview lost its harshness. Maybe Leslie and Paul hadn't perceived anything amiss. Maybe it would still work out. . . .

She bent a little to the side and put her hand into the golden water. It twirled around her hand, cooling, refreshing. Happiness welled up inside her, almost exploding in her chest. Impulsively, she turned to Mick. He was watching her with a slight smile on his lips that showed his dimple clearly. But when their eyes met, it faded and left something a lot more intense, something that suddenly made her breathless and shy.

She dropped her gaze back to the water, not seeing it. *I need to be independent*, she reminded herself.

Having gone in a wide circle, they were now at the end of Elliott Bay, where Puget Sound started. Farther out, Cathy could make out the shore of Bainbridge Island, a long, low formation that seemed to dance above the water.

Mick led the boot in an arc and shut down the motor.

Silence reigned. For a minute, neither moved. Then Mick leaned back, folded his hands across one knee and stared across Puget Sound.

Cathy threw him a glance. His face didn't tell her anything; he seemed to have shut her out. Maybe he was wrestling with his confession, whatever it was. She bit her lips. Now that they didn't move anymore, she could feel the sun-baked wood beneath her legs warming her.

The air smelled of tang and salted water. A seagull shrieked. Cathy inhaled until she could almost feel the air in the tips of her toes. What a perfect place for a romantic date. Maybe he took his girl here too. She probably worked again tonight. Cathy rubbed her shoulder and threw another glance at Mick. What would he confess?

Mick seemed to shake himself with those lionlike movements she was getting to know, then jumped right into the explanation he had promised.

"If I don't want to appear to you like a lunatic, I have to dig out some history." He tilted back his head and looked at the sky. "My mother was never alone. She married my father when she was nineteen, straight from home."

He stopped and brushed his hair away from his face. "The marriage lasted awhile. I guess it wasn't worse than many other marriages, but in the end, they found it didn't work out. When they separated, she just had to take a pick from her many friends who were lining up, waiting for her. When her second marriage broke up some five years later, David married her almost immediately."

He glanced at Cathy, then out to the bay. "I hope he'll last. He's a nice guy." With a sigh, he continued, "So you see, she cannot imagine that life without a partner is worthwhile. She has never lived alone; and she never wanted to. For her, it's a sorry state, a horrible fate only for jerks who fail to find anybody at all."

Mick paused. With a visible effort, he faced Cathy and looked her full in the eyes. "You've just gotten to know my mother. She's a lovely woman—don't get me wrong—but rather overpowering at times."

His jaw clenched when he continued. "I broke off with my last girlfriend two years ago. Frances started to throw hints soon afterward. Was there no girl I would like to present to her? Was there a hidden love in my life? It drove me wild. I was quite happy to be alone for a while, but she didn't believe me. I tried to shut her out, but it didn't work at all. When months passed by, she really started to worry. Secretly, she tried to fix dates for me with the daughters of horrible friends of hers."

Cathy swallowed. How well she understood him.

He shook his head in thought. "When I finally discovered what was going on, I was livid. But it got worse. Half a year later, she thought I'd turned gay. Started to read a lot of literature, asked me funny questions and battled her way through to understanding that I was different."

Cathy couldn't help it, she had to smile.

He saw it, and one corner of his mouth lifted in a lopsided grin. "I know. It sounds preposterous." He sighed. "It didn't help when I assured her I was not gay but had simply not found the right woman yet. For her, that was impossible to understand. She'd had five men lined up at any given moment in her life—without ever raising as much as a little finger."

He leaned back and put his hands onto the wooden planks. The sky started to change from rose to red. "It was the last straw when my sister and David started to talk about understanding my being gay too. I just couldn't stand it. So . . ." He smiled like a boy who'd done something forbidden. "I invented a girl."

"You what?" She couldn't have heard him correctly.

"I invented a girl."

A motorboat sped by with a roar and made their nutshell of a boat sway with the waves it left in its tail.

Cathy clutched at her wooden seat and stared at him.

Mick grinned. "I put her at a safe distance several hundred miles away. Then I told my mother I had met her through the Internet and she had such a brilliant job she couldn't possibly quit and join me here."

"And she swallowed that?" Cathy's eyes turned round.

Mick nodded. "You see, she's rather taken up with herself and has a lousy memory for most things."

Cathy swallowed. "That's a pretty horrible way to describe one's mother."

He shrugged. "It's the truth." Then he lifted his eyebrows and faced her. "Would you have preferred me to gloss it over?"

Cathy rubbed her shoulder, then shook her head. "No."

He smiled. "I thought so. You seem to be an outspoken person." There was so much warmth in his smile and a sort of companionship that something frizzled through her like champagne. To hide her confusion, she swiveled around and focused on the fiery red sun, sinking into the water. The air was light and soft like a transparent blanket, still warm, even though dusk was falling now.

"So when she saw us together, she naturally jumped to the conclusion you were that girl."

"And now she expects me to come to her birthday party tomorrow." Cathy sighed. If only he knew how much she understood. Frances reminded her of a butterfly. A happy-go-lucky life that never touched deep things—though she obviously adored her son.

"I'll work out some excuse," she heard him say.

Cathy shifted her weight on the seat. It seemed cruel. Frances had been so happy. "She'll be so disappointed."

"I know." Mick sighed. "I hate the thought. If only she had given us the time to explain! But that's typical. She breezes in, takes a notion into her head, and it takes more than I know to ever get it out again." He sounded bitter.

"But on the other hand, she's warmhearted, generous, and utterly charming," Cathy said.

He drew his hand through his hair. "That's what makes it so difficult. No matter what I do, I end up feeling like a jerk. If I give in, I play the game and despise myself for it. But if I try to get through to her, I have to become almost violent, and I know it hurts her."

He had described her feelings exactly. Cathy stared at him, bereft of speech.

All of a sudden, he fixed his gaze on her and said, "I've never discussed this before. You must think I'm crazy, schizophrenic or something."

"On the contrary." Her voice sounded curious. "There is nothing more difficult than to take a stand if you don't wish to hurt the other."

"So you do understand." He sounded surprised.

"I do." She had a bitter taste in her mouth.

The last red rays of sunlight reflected in the calm water. It was hard to make out the expression on his face. They were quiet for a long time. A seagull darted ahead close to the shore, its cry sounding like a reproach. They could see it as a black shape before the dark blue sky before it dropped lower and was swallowed by the shadow of the land. The skyline of Seattle came to life. A million little lights, defining the shape of the skyscrapers, were switched on one by one. Their reflections danced on the dark blue surface of the water. To the right and the left, the lights slung lower and appeared as a dotted line all along the coast, twinkling through the darkness.

Cathy felt the tension slipping from her. It was fine. Others were fighting the same demons. She would win, one way or another. The soft breeze caressed her bare arms and her cheeks. "I love this hour." She leaned back and trailed her hand once again through the cool water. "When the light is transparent blue, and it's not quite night yet. Do you often go out with your boat?"

"In summer, at least twice a week. When I'm out on the Sound, I can relax. My best ideas are born right here." He turned his head. "How about you? Where do you have good ideas?"

Cathy grinned. "You'll laugh about me."

"Will I? Why?"

"Because it sounds so . . . so romantic, the way you describe it. In contrast, I have a rather prosaic muse."

She heard the smile in his voice. "So where does your prosaic muse meet you?"

Cathy laughed. "When I brush my teeth."

"But how practical."

"I'm a practical person."

"Are you?" His voice sounded soft. "And sweet too."

Cathy felt a hot wave mounting to her face. Had she heard him correctly? "Mick, why do you call your mother Frances?"

He shrugged. "She asked me to, when I turned fourteen."

Cathy blinked. "Why?"

"Because it dated her. I looked older than fourteen."

"It's true she looks much too young to be your mother. But didn't it hurt?" Cathy remembered how often she had wished she could call someone Mom again.

He stretched. "No, funny enough, it didn't. We were used to her taking whims." He paused, then added, "Cathy?"

"Yes?"

"You don't seem to be shocked by my tale."

Cathy smiled. "I'm not shocked. I understand."

"I'd never have thought I would ever tell anybody. Thank you for listening." His whiskey voice made her spine tingle. All at once, she was short of breath. To cover her confusion she said, "You're lucky Frances didn't take it into her head to see your invented friend on a surprise visit."

Mick chuckled. "In that case, I would have arranged a speedy separation."

Cathy wished he would chuckle more often. She looked across at the lighted skyline. "It's night already," she said. "Look, now all the lights are on."

Suddenly, she sat up with a sharp movement. "Oh dear! I forgot! Where am I going to stay tonight?"

He turned his head to her. His dark voice was full of amusement when he replied, "If you want to, you can stay at my house."

Cathy hesitated. The laugh in his voice became more pronounced, but his face was almost hidden by darkness. "After all, you trusted me with your purse and all its contents. Is this one more difficult?"

"Of course it is," she replied with all the dignity she could muster.

"I'm glad to hear you have some sense of protecting yourself." He took her hand and put something into it.

Cathy closed her fingers around it. It was hard and flat, with sharp edges.

"This is the key to my house," he said. "In summer, I often sleep outside, in a hammock. If we're treated to warm nights, that is. Lock the door, then you'll be safe."

Cathy felt herself blushing and was glad he could not see it. "Okay." She wondered if she had just made a big mistake.

The car rushed through the night. Trees loomed above, then jumped back from sight, replaced by street lamps.

Shadows of houses lining the street showed against the night sky, silent, indifferent. Darkness and light flickered alternately across the dashboard, across his face, across his hands holding the wheel.

There is nothing as intimate as driving through the night in a car. Cathy rubbed her shoulder. It was like sitting in a shell, safe from the outer world, projecting yourself through a foreign landscape. It was funny she felt so at ease, trusted him without hesitation. With the vague idea that it might be good to know where they were heading, she asked, "Where do you live?"

"Northwest Esplanade," Mick said. "It's just a few minutes' drive. We're almost there."

"I like that word, Esplanade."

"It sounds grand, doesn't it?" Cathy saw a depreciating smile before the darkness hid his face again. "But the property only exists due to some mistake in early maps. It seems an office clerk made a calculating mistake that wasn't noticed until years later. When the Northwest of Seattle got popular, they hurriedly declared it to be an independent property. Though that's pure flattery, really." With a flick of his wrist, he turned the car down a gravel drive and cut the motor.

It was the tiniest house she had ever seen. Made of wood and painted in barn red with white window frames, it looked like a house a little girl had dreamed up. A porch surrounded it, covered by a roof of weather-beaten gray shingles. It looked as if it offered as much room as all the space inside.

The house was cleverly illuminated by spots hidden beneath bushes in the garden. Only one lamp was visible. It glowed above the slim wooden door through the soft summer night, and Cathy could see moths twirling around it.

Mick opened the door to his house and stepped to the side to allow her to go in. Cathy gazed around her. She stood in a living room cum kitchen. There was an open fireplace at one side, blackened from smoke, with two easy chairs in front. The cushions were faded red and matched the rug on the floor. Along the left wall she could see a stove, a small fridge, and some cupboards, separated from the living room area by a bar with high stools. Two doors, painted white, were leading off the room at the other end. Mick pushed both open. "Bedroom. Bathroom."

"It's enchanting." Cathy took a step forward.

He threw her a look she could not read, as if he was astonished. But he didn't say anything and went to the fridge with swift steps. "Would you like something to drink?"

Cathy resisted her impulse to go over and peer into the fridge. She didn't know him all that well. "Yes, please. What do you have?"

Mick hesitated. "Well. Beer and Coke."

Cathy had to laugh. "And some ice?"

He returned her smile. "Of course."

"Then I'll take tap water with ice."

His eyes widened in horror. "Are you sure?"

"Positive."

As he filled their glasses, she went to the bedroom and dropped her handbag on the bed. A pile of expensive-looking books with glossy colors was lying next to it. She read the title of the first one. *Making the Most of Small Gardens.* Yes, he'd mentioned he was a gardener, hadn't he?

He didn't have to tell her no woman lived here. The interior was rather spartan. Though he had a red-and-white star quilt as a bedcover. "That's a wonderful quilt," she called through the open door to him.

"It's a gift from Angie."

"Angie?"

"My sister." He came to the door and passed her the cold glass. "I made up the bed this morning. But if you need anything to change tonight or tomorrow, serve yourself." He nodded toward a closet, built into a niche in the wall.

Cathy grinned. "It'll be way too large, but I appreciate it."

Mick hesitated, then said, "Would you like to sit outside for a moment? These summer nights don't come often. I hate to miss a single minute."

"I'll join you immediately." Cathy took her mobile phone out of her bag. "But first, before I forget, I have to call my boss to tell her I won't come in the day after tomorrow."

When she had left her message on the company answering machine, she dialed Dan's number. She was lucky; she only got his mailbox and rattled off without taking a breath, "Hi, Dan. I just wanted to say it's so nice with Mary-Lou, I'll stay over for two more days. Talk to you soon." She hung up, feeling like a louse. She'd never lied to him before. How she hated it. She had to change it. Soon. If only the job interview had gone better. Then she could have faced him with something definite. She pushed the thought away from her and hurried outside to join Mick.

She found him in the back of the house. Two Adirondack chairs sat side by side on the porch and faced the garden. In the corner, just beneath the hammock, a large lantern illuminated the darkness with its soft light. Cathy looked around. The garden lay in darkness, rustling and whispering with the sounds of the night. Farther below, she could hear the murmuring sea.

"If you wish, you can sit here." Mick threw a cushion onto the Adirondack chair next to him. "Did you bring your water? Good."

Cathy fell into the chair and put up her legs. "Hey, they're real comfortable."

"That's why they're here." He grinned. "I even have a small folding table so we can have breakfast outside, if we want to. It's not entertaining in royal style because it's kind of difficult to eat in a reclining position, but for a snack, it's okay."

"It sounds lovely." Cathy smiled at him.

His lion-eyes held hers. Something warm tingled through Cathy. With an effort, she looked away. "I've never seen so many stars before."

"You should see them on a clear night in winter.

Sometimes, you think they'll come down and touch you if you look a little longer."

Cathy smiled. "You love your house, don't you?"

"Yep." For some reason, his voice sounded defensive.

All at once, she heard herself telling him about her parents' house and described her bedroom and the orange curtains with large green apples she had loved so much. He didn't know it was a first for her. Ever since her parents' death, she had tried to shut out the memory knowing it would overwhelm her if she let it come too close. But now, it didn't hurt; instead, it was a relief. Cathy shook her head and wondered at herself.

It was so easy to talk to him; as if they'd known each other since kindergarten. Cathy enjoyed listening to his whiskey voice, enjoyed the feeling of being welcome, of being happy.

"I had a small hut in a tree when I was small," Mick said. "I loved it and hid all my treasures there." He smiled. "Size-wise, my house hasn't changed much."

They fell silent. Somewhere a cricket sang. It was easy not to talk. Cathy smiled. With some people she had to talk nonstop to feel comfortable, but with Mick, it wasn't necessary. He wouldn't misunderstand a silence. Cathy stretched herself out and looked at the starlit sky. Maybe she should tell him about her quest for independence. He would understand. But hadn't she promised herself she would make it all on her own? Without the help of anybody else?

And yet, here she was just a few hours of liberty later

ready to—how had Mick called it?—"hand over." She was too used to it. No, she would hold her tongue and manage on her own. She absolutely had to prove to herself she could do it. Though it was so tempting to just let go and share the burden. Cathy couldn't remember when she had last felt so much at ease with anybody.

In spite of it all, she locked the door when they had said good night, though she felt rather silly. If anybody had proved he could be trusted, it was Mick, wasn't it?

She was so tired she dropped to sleep the minute her head touched the cushion.

The next morning, she woke early. A blackbird was singing, deliriously happy, in a bush next to her window. Remembering how she came to be here, she stretched until her toes tingled.

Why did she feel as if the day would only bring good things? Her car was wrecked, the job was probably lost, and Dan . . . oh, she wasn't going to spoil the day by thinking about Dan. She was wide-awake now.

She sat up, angled for the blouse she had worn yesterday and put it on. At least it was long enough to look decent. Her bare feet made a padding sound on the wooden floor when she went to the kitchen to make coffee. Then she unlocked the front door and returned to the bedroom. She eyed her business suit of the day before and decided she couldn't bear it another minute. A hunt through Mick's drawers unearthed a dark green T-shirt and a pair of shorts she could hold up with a belt. With these treasures, she conquered the bathroom and took a long shower. When she had brushed her hair, she almost felt human again and ready to meet Mick.

But when she ventured out to the little porch, the hammock at the corner was empty. She stopped, insecure about what to do.

Chapter Four

"Good morning."

Cathy swung around. Mick was sitting on the railing of the porch, his hair standing up on top.

Her heart beat a little faster.

Mick jumped from the railing. "I thought I'd dreamed you."

She smiled. "I hope it wasn't a nightmare."

His eyes never left her face. "No. What have you done to your hair?"

Cathy touched her hair. "Why, nothing."

"It looked different last night," he said. "You had it up. I'd never have guessed it would be so long."

"Yes, it coils up well." She grinned. "Very useful if I want to leave a professional impression."

* * *

They were having breakfast on the porch when the sound of a car came up the lane. Mick cocked his head. "Oh no, that's Angie. I forgot she said she would come by early today."

He had barely finished speaking when a slim woman rushed around the corner and came to the porch. A transparent shawl was flying behind her, swinging with every move. When she saw Cathy, her eyes widened, and she stopped dead. Mick grinned. "Angie, stop gaping and come closer. I want you to meet Cathy."

Cathy jumped up and stretched out her hand, wondering if that was too formal. But she couldn't bring herself to just nod. It seemed so stuck-up. Angie gripped her hand with surprising strength and blurted out, "So you do exist? I'd never . . ." She stopped herself and blood rushed up her cheeks. "I'm sorry. I didn't want to sound rude."

Cathy had to smile. Angie wasn't quite as beautiful as her mother, but she had the same delicate features and a laughing mouth. Her brown hair was tied back in a ponytail, swinging along with the shawl.

Mick got up. "Sit down, Angie."

"Can I have something to eat too?" Angie dropped into Mick's chair. "I'm starving."

Cathy hid a smile. Angie had a funny way of emphasizing random words that conveyed a sense of urgency and intensity with every sentence, even if it was completely banal.

"Sure." Mick nodded. "I'll get you a plate and a knife."

"So you're Minnie." Angie smiled at Cathy. "I'm glad I can finally get to know you."

Cathy was thrown off her stride. Fishing for something diplomatic to say, she said, "Usually I'm called Cathy."

Angie blinked. "But Mick always said . . ." She stopped, then her face cleared. ". . . Oh, I know, it's his nickname for you."

"No, it's not." Mick had come up behind her and placed the knife and plate on the small table. Then he looked at Cathy. "I think it's best if we tell her the whole story. Do you agree?"

Cathy nodded. She always preferred the truth. And it wasn't her story anyway.

Mick sat on the railing of the porch and stared into the garden. The house sat on a low cliff by the sea. Wind-beaten and salty, it wasn't ideal for plants, but Mick had made the most of it. By the porch there were rambling roses, a profusion of white and dark red blossoms climbing up the railing and the pillars of the porch. Their colors matched the paint of the house, and now, in full bloom, they seemed to cover the house with a fragile and swinging garment. Cathy got a whiff of their fragrance whenever the breeze moved them with tenderness.

A twisting footpath with white pebbles led the way from the porch to the cragged end of the garden, where the ground fell away and opened the view to the sea. It was bordered by thyme, and to the left and right, there were all kinds of grasses that Cathy had never seen before. They were organized in sweeping curves and moved with every whisper of the wind. Farther out, two giant grasses, almost twice as tall as Cathy, stood as foaming fountains, marking a kind of gate. Seen from the porch, they made an axis that drew the gaze to the sea outside and, farther out, to the fragile-looking blue sky that promised another hot day. From where she was sitting, Cathy could just make out that the path twisted to the side right behind one and disappeared out of sight. An irresistible curiosity made her want to go down there and explore it.

"I met Cathy yesterday in town," Mick said all at once.

Angie dropped her knife. "But I thought you were . . ." Her startled gaze flew from Mick to Cathy and back. "Oh Mickey, I'm so sorry!"

He grinned at her. "There's no need. Minnie doesn't exist."

Angie made a strangled sound that seemed to get stuck in her throat. "What?"

Mick swiveled back to survey the sea. Cathy knew this was the hard part. "I invented her to stop mother from worrying."

"I don't believe that!" Angie's eyes widened.

Mick swiveled around and scanned her face. There was a desperate note in his voice. "You know how she is, Angie."

Angie stared at him. For an instant, the only sound was the swishing of the waves from the other end of the garden. A bumblebee buzzed by, landed on the soft petal of a rose and climbed inside.

"I still don't get it. Tell me again." Angie shook her head. "And make sure you explain it a little bit better."

Mick sighed and told her the whole story.

Angie listened, her eyes riveted to his face. When he had finished, she leaned back. "Wow! If anybody else had told me, I'd have laughed into his face." She shook her head as if to clear it. "I know Frances is difficult," she said. "But to invent a girl is quite another thing! You should stand up to her." All at once, she stemmed her fists onto her hips. "You lied to me too!"

"You believed her when she started spreading the rumor that I was gay."

Angie flushed and started to fidget with the end of her ponytail, which just reached to her shoulder. "Frances told me flat-out it was a fact. At first, I refused to believe her. But later . . ." Her voice trailed off.

Mick sighed. "I don't blame you. She can be so persuasive if she takes a notion into her head. But when some of my friends started to ask me weird questions, I had enough." He grinned. "And that evening of the Shilshole Bay Marina Party, I just couldn't take it anymore. She decided to give me a talk about how much she understood in the middle of the night, and I admit I wasn't all that sober, and so—half as a joke—I said I had a girl called Minnie."

Something in Cathy's brain clicked. "Minnie—like Mickey?"

He grinned at her. "Exactly."

Angie dropped her head in her hands. "I don't believe this."

"And when Frances flung herself on my neck with relief, I couldn't back out anymore."

Angie straightened. "Okay. I understand that." She faced Cathy. "But where do you come in?"

"I came from Spokane yesterday afternoon for a job interview, and in my hurry, I overlooked a stop sign and ran into Mick's van."

Angie's hand flew to her mouth. "Oh no! Where the flowers inside?"

Cathy blinked.

"No, don't worry." Mick grinned. "I collected them later on, after the accident."

Angie breathed a sigh of relief. "Good." Then she beamed at Cathy. "And it was love at first sight!"

"No!" Mick and Cathy simultaneously shouted.

Angie blushed again. "I seem to put my foot in at every turn." She swallowed. "Maybe I'd better stop talking for today."

"That wouldn't help." Mick's grin robbed the words of their sting. "You'd still get into trouble."

Angie shot him an exasperated look and turned back to Cathy. "I don't understand at all. Can't you explain it to me?"

"She would, if you'd let her get a word in edgewise." Mick still grinned.

Cathy cut in. "I'm afraid it won't get any easier to

believe. You see, I was running late for a job interview when we had the accident, and all I wanted was to get there in time."

"So she handed me her purse, credit card and all, by way of a guarantee that she would be back, and asked me to drive her to her appointment." Mick finished with a flourish.

Angie stared at Cathy. "You never!"

"I did." Cathy made a wry mouth. "And I've never been more relieved than when I saw his van coming up after the interview."

As Angie seemed to be speechless, she continued, "And in order to say thank you I invited Mick out to dinner. That's when your mother walked in."

Angie closed her eyes. "As if Seattle wasn't big enough."

"It was a mistake to go to Gino's. I should have known Frances would pass by. They often do," Mick said. "But we were just around the corner, and I didn't think about it." He slanted a smile at his sister and continued, "You should have seen Frances. The welcome of the long-lost son was nothing compared to it. Cathy and I never got far enough to tell her she has nothing to do with the Minnie story. . . . And now Frances expects her to come a little early for her birthday party to get to know her better."

"Oh, no," Angie opened her eyes wide. "What are you going to do?"

Mick drew his hand through his hair. "I'll have to concoct another tale," he said. "Maybe a sudden illness in the family, so Cathy had to return home without delay."

Angie looked horrified. "Frances will be crushed."

Mick sighed. "I know and I feel terrible. But there's nothing we can do."

"But it's her birthday today!" Angie frowned. "And you know how hard she finds it anyway!"

"Why does she find it hard?" Cathy was intrigued.

Mick said, "It's her fiftieth birthday, and she doesn't want to face it." He pressed his lips together. "But that's not my problem."

Angie rounded on him. "How can you be so heartless? She's our mother, after all!"

Mick's eyes hardened. "You just told me I should make a stand against her."

"But you would hurt her so much!" Angie frowned.

"Isn't it heartless of her too, to press her own set of values on him and not to leave him alone if he chooses to live differently?" Cathy said with more vehemence than she wanted.

The siblings swung around. Angie's mouth dropped open. Mick stared at Cathy, then slowly raised his cup of coffee to her. "You're an angel, you know." There was a note in his voice that made her skin tingle.

Then he faced Angie. "She's right."

Angie closed her mouth with a snap. "She may be right, but I don't believe you should disappoint Frances so much on her birthday. It's egotistic, that's what it is!"

"Well, what do you propose to do, then?" Mick's voice was mild.

Angie didn't hesitate. "You could go to the party and pretend you're together."

"No way!" Cathy shook her head.

"Not on your life," Mick said at the same moment.

"Why not?" Angie warmed to her idea. "It wouldn't be difficult! Nobody knows you, Cathy, and if you agree on some main points beforehand, it'll be easy."

"Well, you might start to consider somebody else's feelings besides Frances'!" The orange flecks in Mick's eyes started to blaze. "You have no idea if Cathy is married or engaged or whatever, and you demand her to fall in with your crazy scheme, just to please our mother! It's preposterous! And you dare tell me I should stand up to her!"

He turned away and rubbed his eyebrows. "I wish I'd never started it."

Angie put a hand on Cathy's arm. "Are you?"

"Am I what?" Cathy blinked.

"Married, engaged, or whatever?"

"Angela!" Mick jumped up. "How dare you!"

Cathy had to smile. "No." She paused. "But maybe Mick is."

Angie's eyes widened. "That would beat it all!" She wheeled around to her brother. "Are you?"

"I don't believe this." Mick pushed back his hair. "What are you? The Spanish Inquisition? No, of course not!"

"That's settled, then," Angie said.

Mick opened his mouth, but before he could utter a word, she continued, "It'll be just for today. Then you'll tell Frances that Cathy had to go home again and you can officially break up in a month or so."

"You've been working at the theater too long." Mick's voice sounded like ice.

Angie lifted her hands. "Mick, you know Frances doesn't mean to be horrible. She loves you. Won't it be possible to play the game for just one day?"

Cathy swallowed. She knew these arguments, oh, how well she knew them.

All of a sudden, Mick looked exhausted.

Cathy jumped up. "May I have a word alone with you, Mick?"

He seemed to be surprised. "Of course."

He took her down the path, toward the giant grasses. When the path turned, they were hidden from view. A teak bench was placed with its back against the giant. Silver gray with age, it offered a view out to the sea. Cathy stopped in front of it and faced Mick. All at once, her heart beat hard against her ribs. She swallowed. "If I ask you something now, will you promise to tell me the truth?"

He frowned at her, then nodded. Though he had his hands in his pockets, she could still feel the tension in him.

Cathy took a deep breath. "Would it be distasteful for you to pretend we're a couple today?"

"Lord, no!" he lifted both hands. "But I don't want to put you in an impossible situation. And I don't want to keep on faking something, just to please Frances. It's bad enough as it is; I don't have to involve you too."

Cathy felt better. "Then . . ." She hesitated. "Maybe that's the best way out. Show her that Minnie exists. It will reassure her you're not gay. And if you break it off later, she'll take some time to hatch another crazy idea."

He stared at her, his mouth a thin line. "I can't ask it of you."

Cathy smiled up at him. "I'm rather in your debt, you know. Besides, I'm not sure how to spend the day otherwise." That wasn't true. She could imagine staying for the rest of the day in his perfect garden. Or going swimming, out there, in the vast blue of the ocean. But she also knew better than anybody else what it meant to be in a jam just because you didn't want to hurt somebody you loved . . . and to know the only alternative was to hurt yourself.

If she was honest, she had to admit she would not have offered to help if she didn't like him. But she liked Frances too, and did not want to be the reason for a spoiled birthday. Maybe she could help to uncoil the situation Mick had worked himself into. It would be nice to manage it for others, even if she did not manage it for herself.

"Cathy." He took her hands. His grip was warm and strong. "Now I'm asking you to tell me the truth. Do you feel obliged to do this?"

His lion eyes almost mesmerized her. "No." She cleared her throat. "I'll be fine." Struggling for a lighter note, she added, "As long as you don't start to tell invented love scenes. Then I'd jump on a table and make a scene that would make her birthday truly memorable."

Mick laughed. "I'll try to keep a grip on myself."

"So I understand you barely know each other?" Angie said.

"Yes, ma'am," Mick replied as if he were a schoolboy. They were back on the porch. The girls were stretched out on the chairs and Mick sat as usual on the railing. Angie had cleared away the breakfast stuff with the exception of the mugs.

Angie grabbed her mug, took a big gulp of coffee and said, "You need a crash course, then."

Alarmed, Cathy glanced at Mick.

He sighed. "Angie, take it easy. Nobody is going to put us through a quiz."

"No, but you have to know the rough outlines of each other's lives." Angie shook her head. "Imagine, if somebody walked up to you and said, 'Does your girl love shopping as much as mine does?' You wouldn't know what to say."

"That one is easy," Mick said. "I have yet to meet a woman who doesn't like to shop." He smiled at Cathy, and for no reason at all, she felt as if they belonged together, making a private joke nobody else would understand.

She grinned. "I hate to admit it right now, but I love to go shopping."

Angie cut in, "Any other likes and dislikes?"

Cathy giggled and said the first thing that came to her mind, "I like oranges."

"Wonderful," Mick said. "And we got to know each

other while chatting on the Internet about the growing of orange trees in the Pacific Northwest."

Cathy chuckled. "Is it hard to do?"

Mick shrugged his shoulders. "It depends. You have to keep them in tubs, keep them warm, not too humid, not too dry, for winter you need a light, warm spot . . ."

Cathy held up her hands. "That's enough. When I heard about that, I decided to keep on spending most of my salary on oranges instead of growing them on my farm."

"Do you have a farm?" Angie reacted like a hound to scent.

"No." Cathy grinned. "Of course not."

"She's a businesswoman," Mick said. "I know that much without your precious crash course."

". . . and I fell in love with him because he described the oranges so poetically." Cathy grinned.

Angie laughed. "Mick could not describe anything poetically if his life depended on it."

"Oh?" Cathy raised her eyebrows. "Well, maybe he never saw any need to become poetic with you."

Mick broke into laughter. "She doesn't need to know anything about me, Angie, if she can look as haughty as that."

Angie sighed. "I only meant it for your best, but if you don't want it . . . After all, you're supposed to be a couple since half a year or so. One does get to know the other in six months."

Cathy bent forward and took her hand. "Sorry. I couldn't resist, but of course you are perfectly right. It's just rather difficult to present your life in a nutshell, out of the blue."

"Well, you had a job interview yesterday," Angie said. "Just imagine you have another one."

Cathy shuddered.

Mick said quickly, "I'm twenty-nine. Born in Seattle. One sister, two years older. My parents separated when I was eighteen. Since it was an amicable parting and they had lived different lives for so long, it didn't hit me too hard. I hated school, but love my job. I like spicy food and swimming." He stopped and said, "I can't think of anything else."

"Great," Angie said, "This is about as informative as the entry form for military service."

Cathy threw her a mischievous glance and started in the same vein, "I'm twenty-six. Born in Reading, that's close to London. That's why I still have an English accent. One older brother. My parents were killed in a car crash when I was nine. We came over here to live with my father's brother in Spokane." She stared at the table-top for a second, then continued, "I liked school, and like to work. I used to play softball. Oh, and I go running at least twice a week."

There was a pause.

"I'm sorry about your parents," Mick finally said with his whiskey voice.

"But at least you still had your brother. I bet it helped a lot," Angie said.

Sure. He's my biggest help and my biggest handicap. Cathy jumped up. "Anybody want more coffee?"

Angie glanced at her watch. "Gosh, I've got to run! I only came to collect the keys for the car, and now look at the time! I'll see you two later!"

She ran down the porch, into the house, reappeared a minute later and ran to her car while waving like crazy. Her shawl fluttered behind her.

Mick sighed. "She's not always very sensitive, I'm afraid."

Cathy smiled. "If you ever get to know my family, you won't apologize for yours anymore."

"I think Cleopatra's underwear will be just the thing." Angie's voice came muffled from between the hangers. They were in the theater, looking for something to wear for Cathy. It had been Angie's idea, after they had realized that Cathy couldn't buy anything suitable due to the holiday.

"Cleopatra's what?" Cathy blinked.

"Underwear." Angie's head disappeared between a wolf costume and a ball gown made of pink taffeta. The afternoon sun slanted into the high windows. In the streaks of light, Cathy could see dust dancing.

"It's got to be somewhere here. . . . Yes!" Angie emerged with a long, green dress. She shook it out and checked it with an intent gaze. "Try that on. There's a mirror over there."

Angie handed her the dress, pranced to the door and flicked on a few switches. The room was flooded with light. Cathy held the dress to her neck and went to the mirror while Angie rushed to a box and took out a cushion with needles that she fixed on her wrist.

"Yes!" Angie appeared behind her. "I knew it would match the color of your eyes."

She watched while Cathy put it on, and then, without warning, she changed into the professional dressmaker she was. Gone were the jerky, hectic movements. "I'll tighten it a little at the waist. I'm glad you're so slim; I don't have to let out the seams anywhere."

Cathy usually described herself as flat in front and back and would have preferred to be a little rounder in places, but she wasn't going to admit that. While Angie mumbled and pushed her to and fro, Cathy stared at her face in the mirror. It was true, the green shade was just right for her eyes and the blond hair. But it couldn't take away the freckles and—worst of all—it didn't hide the nose. If only she didn't have that little snub nose. She would be quite passable otherwise.

"That's it." Angie stood up from the floor, put her head to one side and scrutinized Cathy. Then she smiled. "You look lovely."

It was a sleeveless dress, sweeping down to her ankles in one deceptively simple line. Somehow, Angie had managed to hint at a seducing silhouette, promising something without making anything visible.

"It's nice." Cathy was surprised.

"Of course it is!" Angie grinned at her. "I'm not the head dressmaker at this theater for nothing. And now the finishing touch."

Her eyes searched the room, then she hurried to a chest in a corner and started to rummage around. "It's a leftover from *The Dying Swan.* It'll be perfect if the night gets cooler."

She took out a short, white jacket, with luxurious white fur on the collar and at the end of the long sleeves. "It's all fake, of course, as is everything at the theater." She grinned. "But it'll look stunning."

Cathy eyed the jacket with doubts. "Isn't it rather grand?" she asked.

Angie threw her an amused glance. "There'll be two hundred and fifty guests at the party tonight. Frances has decided it's going to be the party of her life, since she has to face it anyway."

Cathy dropped down on the chest. "I had no idea!" Her voice sounded faint. "I thought it was a family event."

"Oh, it is, more or less." Angie waved a hand. "All her ex-husbands with former and current families will come. Frances has kept a good relationship with all of them. In addition, all her friends will be there." She frowned, then said, "Though maybe I should say Frances *believes* she has a good relationship with all her ex-husbands. She's sometimes a little reluctant to face realities."

Cathy's throat tightened. She felt ridiculous. "She would never even notice if I don't show up."

"Oh, yes, she would." Angie nodded her head. "Besides, she asked you to come early to make the most of you."

Panic seized Cathy. "I need to talk to Mick." She jumped from the chest. "This changes everything."

"Mick is busy with the flowers." A flicker of apprehension crossed Angie's face as she took Cathy's hand. "Don't worry, that's only stage fright. We'll help you. It'll work out as smooth as cream. We'll never leave your side."

Chapter Five

Cathy had no chance to speak to Mick alone until they were in the van driving to his mother's. At first, she couldn't bring herself to broach the subject. It seemed so natural to be with him. She stared out of the window and tried to collect her courage. They took the second exit off I-90 and ran south on Island Crest Way, bisecting Mercer Island almost all the way down. Large trees shaded well-kept lawns that seemed to stretch forever. Sometimes she was allowed a tantalizing glance through the lush green, revealing a stately home painted in brilliant white, sometimes only a closed iron gate was on offer, flanked by pillars with acorns or lions on top. This was not a neighborhood where you could open your front door with bare feet.

"We're almost there," Mick said.

He hadn't told her Frances lived in a kind of semi-castle, but she should have guessed it, at the latest after having had a closer look at David. She had to confess her fears. Now.

"Mick."

"Yes?" he smiled at her in a way that almost made her forget what she wanted to say.

"I . . . I'm not sure I can go through with our project."

Mick didn't reply, but he flicked on the turn signal and stopped the car at the edge of the road, right beneath a huge Douglas fir. Then he cut off the motor and turned to her. "What happened?" he asked in his calm way.

Cathy kneaded her hands. "Angie told me there'll be two hundred and fifty people at the party tonight."

He nodded. "Yes?"

She scanned his face. "That's an awful lot. I had no idea."

He appeared to be surprised. "Does it make a difference? I'm sorry, I guess I should have told you. It's just so natural for us. Frances always has huge parties. She has talked about this one for ages, so I just took it for granted."

Cathy nodded, feeling dazed. "But . . ." Her voice trailed off.

"What is it?" His voice was concerned.

How could she tell him? She swallowed but didn't manage to bring out a word.

A Jaguar flashed by, next a Mercedes. Their airstream rattled the windows of the van.

"Cathy." He reached over and took her hand. "Can we make a deal? To keep sane in the middle of this camouflage? Will you promise to always tell me what you think? And I will do the same?"

His clasp was firm, yet light. Cathy nodded and cleared her throat. "Okay." She took a deep breath. "I . . . I didn't know you would present me to so many people. It makes it so official. It'll be all over town tomorrow."

He seemed to be puzzled. "Yes. Is that a problem?"

"Not for me," Cathy hastily replied. "But you have to continue to live with these two hundred and fifty people, and I didn't know that when I persuaded you to agree. I . . . I feel pretty rotten about it, as if I trapped you. I had no idea it would have that scope. Nor that it would be so grand."

He grinned, the dimple in his cheek showing clearly. "I don't exactly live with these two hundred and fifty people, so that's fine. In fact, I do hope what you said will come true. Frances will relax a little, and life will be easier afterward. So I'd rather continue now." He stopped and drew his eyebrows together. "But if you don't want to, we can cancel the whole thing."

Cathy felt as if she had to jump from a high cliff. Finally, she took a deep breath. "No. I'll go through with it." Then she added with a small voice, "Though I'm so nervous, I could eat my shoes and never notice it."

He laughed. "That makes two of us."

Mick started the motor again. When he had filed into the street, he asked, out of the blue, "Do you want kids?"

"What?" Cathy was stunned.

"I'm sorry," Mick said. "I just realized I haven't asked you yet, and Frances is likely to spring it at you."

Cathy had a sudden image of a small girl with lion-brown eyes and blond hair in pigtails, hopping through a garden full of swishing grasses. Hastily, she called herself to order and replied, "Yes, I think I do. Though not yet." She searched his face. "And you?"

He nodded. "I'd like to have kids." He glanced at her. "Preferably with freckles and a nose similar to yours."

"My nose!" Cathy was dismayed. "The poor kids!"

"Your nose was the reason why I accepted your crazy idea to drive you to the interview instead of going to the police." He grinned and stepped up the speed.

"My nose?" Cathy's eyes widened. "You must be joking!"

"No." He smiled. "Has no one ever told you it gives your face a certain sauciness . . . like an elf or a pixie?"

Cathy caught her breath. To hide her confusion, she rushed out the question she'd been wanting to ask before he confused her with his question about kids. "Is there anything I should know about your family? Anything I shouldn't do or say?"

He laughed. "Frances would say no, there's not a blessed thing on earth wrong with us. She's great at walking in a fog she can color any way she likes, preferably rose."

"And what would you say?"

He took a deep breath. "Well. With two ex-husbands

plus their families around, I don't think it's as free of emotions as Frances fondly believes. My father, for one . . ."

"Yes?"

Mick drew his hand through his hair. "I don't know why he shows up at all. He hates parties. But he's always there, sitting on the side, watching all and sundry. Sometimes, he reminds me of a volcano. Gentle on the outside, but you don't know what's going on inside." He shook his head. "Now, Greg, Frances' second husband, is a different caliber. He'll flirt with every woman around, will get stone drunk, and then he'll fall asleep somewhere."

"Sounds great."

Mick grinned. "Doesn't it?"

"And how about David?"

"It's hard to make out David. He seems to be relaxed with all those ex-husbands cluttering the house, but I've often wondered if that's for real."

"So between a volcano, a leer, and an unknown card that might turn out to be anything, we're going to have a lovely time."

His smile was rueful. "I shouldn't have told you. Don't worry, it's not going to touch you. On the surface, they're all friendly."

Cathy had a funny feeling in her stomach.

Mick turned the car into a sweeping drive lined by two low rows of box trees. Immediately behind them, dark red roses formed a parallel line. They foamed up like a crest of wave behind the box as if it was bent on rolling over it within the next second. Cathy gasped with delight. "It looks as if it were alive and moving!"

He smiled, but said nothing.

"Cathy!" Frances welcomed her with outstretched hands and enveloped her in a cloud of perfume that made Cathy think of a glittering Paris at night. Their cheeks touched light as butterflies. Then she turned to Mick and smiled up at him. The high door framed her slim figure to perfection. "Mickey."

"Happy Birthday, Frances." Mick hugged her.

"I'm so glad you came early." Frances emerged from the hug with a swimming movement and kept right on talking. "Can you imagine they took the trees in the tubs you brought and placed them at all the wrong places? Could you be a darling and make it right? And tell the caterer the dessert should *not* be on the table right from the start? There's a problem with the electricity too, the spots are not working as they should, and someone put them on the front porch, but it's the terrace that needs to be illuminated!"

She led them through an entrance hall that would have accommodated the whole of Mick's house. Cathy swallowed. The high walls were built in an octagonal form and covered with wallpaper that shimmered like light green silk. Right across from the entrance, a stairway swung upward to the gallery in one graceful curve. Above them, a chandelier that could dwarf a small sailboat caught the low rays of the sun and reflected the dancing light onto the green walls. A creamy colored marble floor with intricate inlays stretched in front of them. *These riches would crush me.* Cathy stepped a little closer to Mick. *Unless I'm allowed to skid across the floor in soap bubbles.* She smiled to herself.

Suddenly, she spotted a vase and forgot everything around her. It was higher than any vase she had ever seen, reaching to her shoulders. Made of almost translucent porcelain, it was filled with two matching tree boughs, covered by tiny blossoms so pure and white they didn't look real. Cathy touched one with her finger tips. It had a velvety touch. Their soft fragrance made her lightheaded. "They're exquisite."

Frances laughed. "Yes, aren't they lovely? As Mick's girl, you'll soon get used to the most beautiful flowers."

Cathy hoped Frances didn't notice her blush. She felt conspicuous, as if everybody could see at a glance they were only faking it.

They crossed a dining room where you could entertain a king and his guests at a moment's notice and left the house by way of high French doors.

A perfect lawn stretched in soft waves down to the wooden jetty, where several teak lounge chairs invited you to forget the worries of the world. The water of Lake Washington glittered in the sun. To the right, Cathy saw the edge of a pool through some tall maple trees. She felt much better outside.

Frances took them to a deep seating sofa in a corner of the terrace. The sofa and several cubic chairs were all grouped around a low coffee table. They were padded with cushions so thick and white, they looked like fluffy clouds. With an elegant movement, Frances subsided into one of them. Cathy felt out of place in Mick's shorts and T-shirt. She glanced at him. At least he wore a casual shirt too, with shorts and loafers. Frances, in contrast, was in a short gown that floated around her well-shaped body unsubstantially like a well-behaved cloud.

"Would you believe it, the caterer said he could not get crab meat, but I love it so much, so I told him I don't care how he manages it, but I simply expected him to bring some." Frances bent forward and gestured at a tray with drinks. "Would you like some iced tea or lemon water, Cathy? Or anything else?"

"Iced tea, please."

Frances poured her a glass without stopping to speak. "Mick, Dave said you should go and join him, he needs your help with something. I didn't really understand, it's got to do with the parking on the street. Here's your glass, Cathy. Add some lime slices to your drink. They're so refreshing."

Mick struggled out of the deep sofa. "All right, I'll go and check it out."

Cathy felt as if her only friend was leaving her alone with a hurricane. Something must have shown in her face, because he went to her, touched her shoulder and said, "I'll be back in a second," and disappeared.

Cathy took a large gulp of her iced tea and just managed not to swallow a lime slice. This was it. Her first test.

Frances beamed at her. "All right, ask me. I'm all yours."

Cathy blinked. She must have missed a vital part of

information somewhere. "Ask . . . what?" A breeze murmured in the trees behind her.

Frances looked surprised. "Well, I'm sure there are thousands of things you'd like to know about Mick."

"Oh," Cathy swallowed. "Right." She hunted for a fitting question. "What . . . what was he like as a kid?"

Frances leaned back in her chair and crossed her legs. "He was a quiet boy, and he always loved flowers and things. I remember one day I came into the garden, and he sat on the terrace steps and cried his heart out. When I asked him what was the matter, he sobbed that his Daddy had murdered all the grass, because he had cut off its head that morning when mowing the lawn." She smiled, lost in memory.

The story came so pat Cathy suspected Frances to have prepared it long ago. It may even have been invented. But in spite of that, she discovered she would like to see a picture of Mick as a boy.

Frances said, "I had a hard time convincing him it was like cutting your fingernails. The grass doesn't feel anything."

"Which may have been a lie," Cathy said, more to herself than anyone, and watched a drop of condensed water rolling down her cold glass.

"Yes, but if so, it was a lie that was necessary!" Frances shook her hair.

Cathy lifted her head. "So you believe some lies are necessary?"

"Oh, absolutely!" Frances took a dainty sip from her glass. "Take some more iced tea, do. How horrible if everybody said the truth all the time!" Her beautiful eyes widened. "Just think how impolite it would be!" Suddenly, she shot a sharp look at Cathy. "Don't tell me you're one of those I-always-tell-the-truth people. I'd never have thought it of you!"

Cathy took a deep breath and rubbed her shoulder. She tried to compose an answer that was both honest and polite, but before she could speak, Frances said, "But no, I can see you're not! You have such a . . . a fun face . . . like a faun or something. You could never be one of those dried-up, serious women."

Cathy swallowed.

Frances threw back her head and laughed. "Really, I can't tell you how happy I am that Mick's girl is so nice."

Mick's girl. There it was again. It frizzled through Cathy like an electric shock and made her fingertips tingle. She was Mick's girl. For one night.

Frances continued, oblivious of Cathy's reaction. "You know, when Mick told me ever so often you had no time to come, I seriously started to worry if you were strange. But now I am reassured, and I'm–oh–so–happy you came as a surprise for my birthday."

Cathy started to feel desperate. Frances' joy at getting to know her had nothing to do with the way she really was. All of a sudden, she understood much better why Mick had found it so difficult to stand up to his mother. How could he, if he never even managed to get a word in edgewise?

Frances said, "It'll be so nice to get ready, all three of us girls together and . . ."

Cathy drained her glass and got up. "When do you think we will start?" She hoped she didn't sound too rude. "Maybe I should go and ask Mick for the keys to the car to get my stuff out?"

Frances smiled. "You don't want to miss him a single more minute than necessary, do you?" With a light movement, she floated up and took Cathy's elbow. "I do understand. Though it's a long time ago." She sighed. "Come on, I'll show you the way."

They found the men on the drive in front of the house, deep in conversation. When they came nearer, Mick looked up. The smile that lit his eyes made Cathy's lips curve automatically in reply.

"Cathy." Dave stretched out his hand to greet her. "How nice to see you." Cathy was surprised his brown hair was streaked with gray. Yesterday, in the restaurant, he had seemed much younger. Then his shrewd eyes met hers, and suddenly, she knew the gray hair was misleading.

He turned to his wife. "We've just about finished, Frances. I told Mick we only have to . . ."

Cathy stopped listening. Mick bent down to her and murmured in her ear, "How did it go?"

Cathy whispered back, "She says I've got a faun's face. Due to that she's sure I can't be as horribly honest as I appear."

"You're kidding."

"No." Cathy's nose touched his ear. All at once, she felt light and happy. She lowered her voice even more. "I do understand the need for Minnie much better now."

"You do?" Mick smiled at her. "I'm glad."

Cathy looked up.

Frances and Dave were watching them with a smile. Cathy could feel herself blushing. Darn. Had they overheard them?

But Frances only smiled and glanced at her slim wristwatch, set with tiny diamonds.

"I think we'll get dressed now. Angie will be here any minute. She promised to help us get ready."

When Cathy descended the steps an hour later, excitement knotted up her stomach. It was easy to feel like a princess when gliding down such a grand staircase in an evening gown. And why not enjoy it, even if it was only borrowed glory?

The gilt-rimmed mirror upstairs had given her a little confidence. Thank God Angie knew so much about dressing . . . and Frances about makeup. When Frances told Cathy to close her eyes and dusted a glittering powder on her face with a fragrant brush, Cathy didn't dare to move an eyelash. There was something about getting ready for a party that merged total strangers together in a way that beat a five-year acquaintance. Provided they were women, of course. Exchanging lipsticks and commenting on bras was just par for the course on a night like this. Cathy wondered if Mick discussed his suit with Dave with as much enthusiasm, and couldn't suppress a grin. She had wanted to pull her hair up, but Angie and Frances persuaded her to leave it down. When Cathy said she would have to peer half-blinded through an impractical curtain of hair all night, Angie agreed to brush the front streaks loosely back and fixed them in a little knot with glittering stones that Frances conjured up from somewhere. The result surprised Cathy so much, she said before thinking twice, "I think Mick will like that."

Angie shot her an amused look and Cathy blushed. To cover her confusion, she said, "Your dress is fabulous, Angie."

It was tight and black and made her look like a supple witch. The inevitable scarf was bound around her neck, today in a vivid red hue, flying with every quick movement she made.

Angie smiled. "Thanks. Bob doesn't even know what he's missing."

"Who's Bob?"

"My boyfriend. He's in Boston this week, on a business trip."

"It's a shame he's not here." Frances threw a luminous white dress over her head. "I believe he could have made it if he had tried harder." She smoothed the soft fabric over her hip.

Angie sighed and pressed her lips together.

Cathy changed the topic and managed to escape a short time later.

At the foot of the steps, a young man stood and stared up at her. He had bulging eyes, but his square chin and broad shoulders helped to distract from them. "Hello, beautiful lady." He held out his hands. Cathy smiled and overlooked the hands. This was too intimate a start for her taste. "Hello," she replied in a tone calculated to cool him off and tried to edge past him.

"My name's Stephen." He stepped into her way.

"I'm Catherine." She made sure there wasn't a trace of warmth in her voice.

Angie appeared at the top step. "Oh, hi, Stephen," she called out loud. "You're early."

"It's worth it, if I can see all the beautiful ladies first." He bowed.

Angie rushed down the steps and took Cathy's arm. "We'll see you later, Stephen. I still have to show a few things to Cathy."

"Phew," Angie murmured as soon as they were out of earshot. "He's a rather dreadful cousin of Frances' second husband, Dick. I avoid him whenever I can." She grimaced. "But of course Frances had to invite him. She believes nobody who belongs to the family can be bad." She peered through the door onto the terrace. "Darn. Where's Frances? She should be out front, welcoming the guests." She swiveled around to Cathy. "Will you excuse me for a second? I have to hunt for Frances, but I'll be back in minute, and I'm sure Mick is around somewhere too." She hurried from the room, the scarf flying behind her.

Left on her own, Cathy sauntered out to the terrace. It was highlighted by the spots that were by now in the right positions. The air was warm and soft. Cathy smelled a whiff of flowers she didn't know. Sweet, a little cloying. Lilies, maybe. With careful steps minding her high heels,

Cathy ambled over the lawn and stopped from time to time to contemplate the sprawling house with every window lit up. It was two stories high and had perfect proportions. Each room had a French window that opened onto a balcony with a wrought-iron parapet. Painted in a buff yellow color, it stood with ease and the quiet assumption of being perfect between four massive maple trees. But in spite of it all, she preferred Mick's house on the cliffs. For some reason, it had felt like home.

Between the trees, she found the pool. It was covered by dozens of swimming candles. Funny, how much atmosphere candles could make, even though it wasn't dark yet, only dusk. So festive.

One burning candle had lost its balance and took in water. Cathy knelt down at the edge of the pool and reached for it. It was too far away, though she missed it only by an inch. Searching in the bushes close by, she found a branch that could help. She retrieved it and returned to the little light.

Bending down again, she persuaded it to come ashore. Then she drained the water from it and straightened the walls with care, to avoid quenching the light. Smiling, she put it afloat once more and watched it sailing away. If only every problem was as easily solved.

When she lifted her head, Mick stood on the other side of the pool, watching her. He wore a tuxedo and looked formidable, almost like a stranger. Cathy's throat constricted, and her heart stopped for one beat. Their eyes met and held. Cathy could hear herself breathing.

And suddenly, she knew what attracted her so much. He was a curious mix of determination and gentleness. He would never shout at you. He would be willing to hear your point, even if he didn't agree. That was why she felt so at ease with him. No matter what happened, he wouldn't walk all over her. And yet, there was also a strength underneath, an independent streak she felt more than she saw it. It was the reason why she kept thinking of him as a lion. A lion conveyed the same impression of controlled strength, of muscles under control, no unnecessary prancing, no vain show-off. Cathy swallowed. The attraction pulled at her and threw her off balance. It was dangerous ground . . . exhilarating too. Cathy couldn't turn away, though she feared he could read her face like an open book.

He came around the pool to join her, his eyes never leaving hers.

A breeze carried the sound of laughter from the terrace and somebody shouted, "Here's to you, Frances!"

All at once, the bubble burst. Of course. This was only a fake. He did it to shake free from his mother . . . and she had put him up to it. It would be the height of impertinence to misuse the situation. After all, he was in no position to say no tonight.

Besides, she had promised herself to become independent. She couldn't break free just to slither straight into another bond. It was high time she proved she could make it on her own. Now was not the time to think about . . . about anything.

Cathy knotted her hands together to stop them from shaking. She had to be neutral. Friendly. Superficial.

Mick stopped next to her, stretched out his hand and helped her up. They stood so close to each other, Cathy could smell his skin, a heady fragrance, mingled with aftershave. If this were for real, she'd . . .

"Cathy." His whiskey voice was warm and dark.

"Yes?" She barely dared to glance up, for fear he would read all she tried to hide.

For once, there was no smile in his eyes. He touched her cheek, a feathery touch that sent a tremor through her whole body.

She'd never felt so confused before.

"Why do you always look like a dream?" he asked. "Sort of transparent. Like a fairy."

"That's the dress." She fought hard to find a lighter note. "Cleopatra's underwear."

He was startled, she could tell by his involuntary movement. "I beg your pardon?"

"Cleopatra's underwear." She laughed. "At least that's what Angie called it." Thank God she had found an easy answer.

His yellow-flecked eyes smiled at her. "No wonder the pharaoh had no eyes for any other woman."

Cathy blushed and tried to give a light answer, but her tongue knotted itself together and refused to work.

He clasped her arm, his fingers barely touching her skin. It was enough to make her shake from head to toe. "Come on, I guess we have to face the lions now. Frances has asked for you."

They strolled back to the illuminated terrace. "How do you feel?" he asked just before they reached it.

"Terrified." Cathy's voice choked.

"Really?" He stopped dead. "Maybe we should pretend even to ourselves it's for real. You know, it feels quite natural to me."

Before she could stop herself, Cathy blurted out, "No!"

He let go of her. His face went blank. "I'm sorry."

Cathy grabbed his arm. "Mick, I'm sorry, it wasn't . . ."

"There you are!" Angie hurried up to them. "Frances wants us to take some family pictures. Please go to the drawing room. I still have to find Dave."

"No!" Cathy lifted both hands. "I can't join you in family pictures!"

Angie's mouth dropped open. She stepped back a pace. "But you have to! Frances would never understand!"

Cathy stared at her, helpless, but before she could say anything else, Mick said, "Run along and find Dave, Angie. I'll talk to Cathy."

Angie hesitated, then nodded and hastened away.

Cathy wheeled around to face Mick. "I really can't!" It sounded like a plea.

He smiled at her, the orange flecks in his eyes almost hidden. "Why not?"

"I'll be history by the time you'll have those pictures developed!" There was a lump in her throat.

He leaned against the low parapet of the terrace, completely relaxed. "If my mother took down all the pictures with ex-husbands in them, she'd have almost none left."

"But I have no claim at all; we're only pretending the whole thing!" She knew her reaction was out of proportion, but she couldn't help herself. She wanted it to be real, but it scared her too.

"I know," he said. "But if we treated it as a nice evening in the company of someone one likes, it's not unethical to have one's picture taken together, is it?"

Her panic abated. "No . . . no, I guess not," she said. "I'm sorry, Mick, I don't want to be difficult."

One side of his mouth lifted in a lopsided grin. "I guess it takes some getting used to for both of us."

With misgiving, Cathy followed him to the drawing room. It didn't feel right. Or rather, it felt much too right. She could so easily become used to being part of this . . . part of him.

It got worse when an uncle—or was it a cousin?—of Mick's told them where to stand and asked Mick to put his arm around her shoulders. She had to resist the urge to snuggle up to him.

"Frances, come a little bit forward. You've got to be more in the center!" The uncle or cousin emerged from behind his camera again and waved his left arm as if he wanted to lose it by the sheer force of his movements. "Dave, step closer to her and try not to look as if we're at a funeral. Angie, you've got to move up. And stop fidgeting. Can't you stand still for a minute, girl? Mick, what have you done to your girl? Has she swallowed a rod?"

Mick laughed and drew Cathy closer. "She's terrified

by your drill, Rick. We'll all look as scared as rabbits by the time you're done." He smiled down at Cathy, and she had to laugh.

When the ordeal was over, Cathy took a deep breath. By then, more guests had arrived and claimed Mick's and her attention.

During the next hour, Mick presented Cathy to so many people, she couldn't remember a single face or name. She was surprised by how easy it was to pose as Mick's girl. Everybody asked the same questions and didn't listen to the answers, so she soon felt at ease and watched the throng of glittering people pass by.

All at once, it occurred to her how how many well-groomed and even beautiful women she had seen . . . as if it had been necessary to attain a certain level of physical beauty before being admitted to the party. She couldn't help but commenting on that when they had a minute to themselves. "Are all these beautiful women the daughters of your mother's friends she has been throwing at your head?" Cathy took a sip from her glass of wine.

He laughed. "Some of them, yes. Why?"

They were on the terrace. Mick had his back to the garden, and the light that came from the high glass doors illuminated his face so she could see his dimple.

"You seem to be rather difficult to please," she said.

He lifted his eyebrows. "Because I didn't want any of them?"

Cathy hesitated. "Yes. They seemed nice. And some were stunning."

Mick shrugged. "They're on the hunt for a rich husband. As soon as I disillusion them, they loose interest."

Cathy gasped. "Surely not all of them!"

A shadow passed over his face. "The one who mattered did."

He smiled at someone over her shoulder and drained his glass. "Shall we go to the buffet now? I'm ravenous."

Cathy knew better than to continue with a subject he had closed. So someone had hurt him. Someone he had loved. She was surprised how fiercely she resented that woman. Did he still love her?

They had just reached the glass doors that led from the terrace into the living room when Frances appeared before them like a fragrant cloud. "Oh, Mick, Cathy, there you are! I've been looking for you for ages!"

Mick stopped in his tracks. "Yes?"

Frances didn't notice the obvious reluctance in his voice. "I want you to meet a friend of mine. She's in my Chinese shadowboxing class. I've just told her your story, and now she would like to meet both of you because she thinks that's so romantic!"

Cathy wished she'd never started the camouflage. But there was no way to back out now. She would ask Mick to take her home as soon as she had a chance.

Home. Mick's house wasn't her home. Nor was it ever going to be because she had to become independent; she had to learn to be free. If only she didn't feel so miserable.

But when she saw the face of the woman who was

keen on getting to know them, she realized worse was to come.

"This is Leslie Peters." Frances put a hand on the arm of a woman with white hair.

Cathy blanched.

Leslie stared at her, surprise written large on her face. "Catherine Albray?"

"Oh!" Frances eyes grew round. "You know each other?"

Cathy drew a deep breath and racked her brain for something clever to say. But the only thing that filled her mind was her own voice, repeating what she had said yesterday afternoon, "No. I don't have any friends in Seattle." And now she was presented as Mick's long-standing girlfriend with such an abundance of family even an Arab sheik would not dare to call it small.

"Yes." Leslie drew out the word. "We met yesterday afternoon."

Mick's eyes narrowed, then he shot a look at Cathy. Thank God he had caught on. David ambled over and joined them in his silent way. He held a small glass with a golden brown liquid in his hand.

Cathy smiled with an effort at Leslie. She had to find a safe topic of conversation. Now. "I didn't know you did shadowboxing," she said. "I hear it's very demanding."

"In the beginning it is." Leslie sounded clipped and precise, not interested in pursuing the subject. "I seem to remember you said you had neither family nor friends in Seattle."

Cathy swallowed, very aware of Frances at her side,

who for once listened with all due attention. "Well, it may not seem like it, but in a way, it's true." How on earth was she going to get out of it?

"But Cathy!" Frances opened her eyes wide. "Of course it's not true, you have loads of—"

"Frances." Mick interrupted her as if he had no manners at all. "Let Cathy explain what she means."

Frances stopped in the middle of her sentence and stared at him, a mixture of surprise and indignation on her face.

Dave lifted one eyebrow even higher than usual.

Cathy knew she had to continue in a rush before Frances could recover. "Frances may have told you I've not been to Seattle before. I met all of them for the first time tonight."

"But you've been Mick's girl for months!" Frances frowned.

Couldn't she hold her peace? "Of course," Cathy gritted her teeth. "But I only found out this afternoon how close to Seattle he lives. I always thought it was at least an hour away."

Gosh, it was the weakest excuse she'd ever heard. Leslie would think her positively dim-witted. Maybe an earthquake would help now, so she could sink into the ground. Just a small one. She drew a deep breath and got a whiff of the liquid in David's glass. Whiskey. She needed one too.

"How long have you been going to classes together?" Mick pitched in.

Frances ignored him. "Cathy, how come you met Leslie? I thought you'd only come for my birthday?"

Cathy swallowed again. "Not quite. I had a job interview at the Seattle Convention Center where Leslie is the chief event coordinator."

David searched her face, a thoughtful expression in his eyes. Cathy cringed. What did he think?

Frances clapped her hands. "But that's famous! So you're finally thinking of getting married!"

Cathy gasped.

Mick was more used to the way his mother's mind worked. "Moving into the same town is not necessarily the first step to the altar, Frances."

But Frances was shining with joy and hugged them both. "Oh, I know, but it's the right step, and I'm so delighted, and you know, you could get married this autumn. . . ." She assessed Cathy. "You'd look lovely in a bronze-colored surrounding, and we would have the reception here and then have dinner at the Queen Anne Restaurant or . . . maybe better, at Salty's. . . ."

"Frances." Mick's voice had an edge Cathy had never heard. "Stop it."

"Or maybe we could ask Gino's brother, he's a great caterer. . . ."

"That's enough." Mick hadn't lifted his voice, but it had a ring of finality in it that chilled Cathy and even went through Frances' armor.

David lifted both eyebrows.

Leslie's eyes swiveled from one to the other, then she

gave a small wave and hurried away. Cathy breathed a sigh of relief.

"But . . . what's the matter?" Frances asked. "Why do you speak to me like that?"

Mick closed his eyes for an instant. "I don't want you to plan my marriage or anything else in my life."

"But I'd never . . . !" Frances lifted both hands.

"Yes, you do all the time. Stop it, or I promise you'll lose me altogether."

Cathy put her hand on Mick's arm, not knowing if it was meant as a support or as a restraining motion.

"How dare you speak to me like that!" Frances turned red. "After all I've done for you! And on my birthday too!"

Mick's eyes darkened.

"Frances." Cathy hurt for them both. "Please let us alone on this. We'll inform you in time, on all you need to know."

Frances swept down on her like a predator, her dark eyes tragic. "I'd never have thought you'd be like that. You seemed to be such a fun person, and now I see you're turning Mick against me."

David frowned and put his arm around Frances' shoulders.

Cathy cringed. Her hand fell from Mick's arm, and she stepped back a pace. Mick grabbed it again and pulled her close to his side. His eyes blazed. "This has nothing to do with Cathy. I should have shown you the limits much sooner."

"Show me the limits?" Frances turned on him like a fury. "I'm your mother!"

"And I'm not a child anymore!"

"That does not mean you can stop being respectful to your mother!" Frances gained back part of her dignity.

"I'm not disrespectful!" Mick's voice lifted. "I am only trying to live my own life."

"Well, you've always done what you thought best anyway." Frances pressed her mouth into a thin line. "And I don't see why the simple mentioning of your marriage should be such an issue."

There was a pause. The murmur of voices and a happy tune floated out of the living room onto the terrace. Cathy tried to breathe again.

"Unless you're pregnant and need to get married immediately?" Frances asked.

David stared at his wife.

Cathy was dumbfounded. She felt Mick's hand tighten on hers.

"Oh, no," he said. Then he took Frances by the shoulders and said, pronouncing each word with care, "Cathy is not pregnant. We will plan our marriage by ourselves. You'll be informed. Stop speculating. Stop planning. Please."

"But . . ." Frances pushed his hands from her shoulder. "I've only asked a harmless question. There is no need to make a big scene. I'd never do anything you don't want, you should know that."

All of a sudden, Cathy was filled with a sadness she'd

never felt before. Here were two people, both lovable, nice people, each loving the other, and yet they were unable to communicate, to truly tell and understand how each felt. She blinked. It was exactly the same with her and Dan. She'd never seen it so clearly before. She'd only known she had to get out. Soon. Having acted by instinct, she now knew her decision had been right, even though it would hurt both of them.

For the fraction of a second, she met David's eyes and, to her surprise, she saw a glimmer of the same understanding there.

"Frances." Her voice sounded small. "Would you like to choose the gown with me? I'd like that. But you'll have to be patient because Mick and I still need some time before settling a date."

She felt Mick stiffen at her side and hoped he was not going to throw her into the pool.

Frances' face lit up. "Oh, Cathy, that's a wonderful idea. What kind of gown are you thinking? A grand one with a hoop or . . . ?"

"I've no idea yet." Cathy felt sweat breaking out. "But there's plenty of time. We can discuss it next year."

Frances was about to reply something, when they heard Angie's voice. "Frances, where are you? Fraaaances!"

"I need to go." Frances spun around and flounced away.

Dave glanced from Mick to Cathy, a half smile on his lips. Then he shrugged and followed her without another word.

"Phew." Cathy couldn't start to guess what Mick was thinking. It took all the courage she had to meet his gaze.

"So we're going to get married in a year, are we?" His voice had a curious tone.

Cathy was glad to see the smile lurking again in those lion eyes. "I'm sorry." For some reason, she was breathless. "We'll have broken up long before that, and at least she dropped the baby idea when I proposed it."

There was a pause. "You're not very good at being cruel, either, are you?" There was a frown on his face but somehow, Cathy got the impression it wasn't directed at her.

"No," she said. "But I'm working on it."

He laughed, then leaned against the wall of the house with a sigh. "It doesn't make sense, now, does it? Why should you need to be cruel to someone you love?"

Cathy hesitated, then said, thinking it out as she said it, "I think it's only if that particular love is too overpowering, too suffocating."

She met his eyes. Suddenly, she wanted to tell him all about her true reasons for coming to Seattle, but she couldn't bring herself to do it here, surrounded by hundreds of people, constantly being prone to interruptions.

"Let's go and eat," she said.

They worked their way to the buffet, stopped by several people on the way, but Mick always continued after a few light words, undeterred like a hound on a scent. The tables where the buffet had been spread were only a few steps away when a voice like dark silk greeted Mick and made him stop in his tracks. He turned around in slow motion. "Nicole. How are you?"

"Just fine." The dark-haired woman was almost as tall as Mick. She had the most perfect skin Cathy had ever seen. Like cream with a drop of cherry juice. Her eyes were dark with long lashes that formed an intriguing shadow in the form of a triangle on her rosy-colored cheeks.

"It's quite some time since we met," she said with her dark voice.

Mick nodded. "I guess so."

Banal words, yet Cathy sensed the encounter was filled with tension. She knew it for sure when Mick turned away from Nicole, stared at Cathy as if he had never seen her before, put his arm around her shoulders and drew her close. He'd kept a careful distance after the pictures, not crowding her, yet not being too far to raise suspicion either. This felt different. She wasn't sure if he used her as a barrier or as a shield, but it made her sad.

"I'd like you to meet Cathy," he said.

Nicole nodded. Her glance felt like an icy breeze. She had a perfect body, full curves, long legs. Cathy felt a stab of admiration. In comparison, she looked like a sparrow. Before Cathy could make a move, David came up from behind. "Mick, could you help me a minute?"

Mick sighed. "We're just on our way to the buffet, Dave, and I'm starving. Could it wait?"

Dave bent forward and whispered something into his ear. Mick sighed. "Oh well, all right." Then he turned to

Cathy. "Will you be an angel and get me something too? I'll be right back." He smiled at Nicole, said, "Bye. I'll be seeing you," and was gone.

Cathy wasted a smile on Nicole, who didn't even twitch a corner of her beautiful mouth in response. Feeling awkward, Cathy hurried to the buffet. She was just loading a second plate with tiny roasted potatoes when Nicole's voice came from behind her. "You can't know him well if you haven't learned he hates potatoes of all kinds."

Cathy swung around to face the snow-white beauty. Smiling with all the sweetness she could muster, she said, "Didn't you know one's taste changes every seven years or so? I'm afraid your information is not up-to-date."

She collected both plates and brought them out to the terrace to a quiet corner where she had seen empty iron chairs. They looked as if they had been shipped over from some castle in Europe. She balanced the plates on one chair, sat down on another, and drew a third one closer for Mick. As she lifted her head, she saw Nicole standing just within the glass doors, watching her.

When Mick appeared several tiny potatoes later, she said in a low voice. "Put on a poker face, will you? Nicole is watching."

Mick didn't bat an eyelid and sat down next to her. "Yes?"

"You love potatoes," Cathy said. "Particularly the ones I put on your plate."

He looked at her, the smile back in his eyes. "Is that so?"

Cathy nodded. "Yes. Nicole was good enough to inform me you can't stand the stuff, and I simply had to say she was wrong."

He smiled. "And now I have to finish them all?"

Cathy grinned. "Yes. Is it very horrible?"

"It is," he said. "But it's for a good cause." He glanced down at his plate and added, "Thanks for bringing something else too."

"The white stuff in that extra bowl is orange mousse with white chocolate." Cathy pointed it out to him. "If you should not want it, I volunteer to finish it off."

He grinned at her. "I bet you do."

"What did Dave have to whisper about?" Cathy asked some minutes later.

Mick swallowed a potato with obvious effort. "Oh, some poor guy got too drunk and . . . well, let's say we helped him get rid of the stuff and put him in a taxi to go home. But I don't think he'd want to broadcast it around."

"I see." All at once, Cathy realized Mick had not touched alcohol the whole night, with the exception of a glass of champagne to toast his mother. "Don't you drink?" she asked.

"I usually do," Mick replied and added hastily, "not to get stone drunk, but I do like beer in summer or a good glass of wine with good food." He looked at her with a curious expression, hesitated, and said, "However, tonight is difficult enough even being sober. I can't start to imagine what might happen if I lost control."

She had finished eating and put her plate on the chair next to her. "What would you do?" she smiled. "Do you think you might start to walk around and tell everybody about our crazy setup?"

He didn't laugh. He met her eyes, then said, "No. I'm afraid I would kiss you."

Chapter Six

Cathy stared at him. Her throat hurt. Finally, she managed to say in a rough voice, "Because Nicole is watching?"

His fork fell to the ground. He didn't notice. "Because Nicole . . ." He swallowed. "So you guessed?"

Cathy's heart sank straight into her stomach and settled there, stone cold. She'd never felt so lonely. "She's the one who mattered."

Mick threw her another of those looks she could not read and put his plate away, almost all the potatoes gone. Then he took her hand. "Let's get out of here." He pulled her up.

Cathy followed, though she would have preferred a hole to hide in.

They were heading for the garden when they were stopped by a man who seemed familiar to Cathy. His black-rimmed glasses blinked in the light. "I haven't seen you all night, Mick." His voice held a plaintive note.

Mick smiled. "I saw you on and off, but always too far away." He put a hand on Cathy's arm. "Cathy, this is my father, Paul Vandenholt. Dad, this is Catherine Albray."

"I'm delighted to meet you," Mick's father shook her hand with astonishing enthusiasm. "Albray, you said? You're not by any means connected with Christopher Albray, the professor who has written that outstanding book on the use of nouns?"

Cathy forced a smile. "He's my uncle." At times, the book had been a more important part of Chris' life than the two children his brother had left him.

"Really." Paul took off his glasses and started to clean them with a tissue he took out of his pocket. "You should have told me, Mick."

Mick's eyes met Cathy's, a hidden laugh deep in them. "I'm sorry, Dad. I never knew you admired any Albray." To Cathy, he said, "Dad is professor at the College of Education, which is part of Seattle University." He smiled at his father. "A passionate professor, I should say."

Cathy couldn't for the life of her imagine how Frances could ever have tied up with this professor. She would never understand the fervor he had for his job, nor he her need for dissipation and amusement. She surveyed him a little closer. He must have been good-looking as a young man. He had broad shoulders and a clear-cut face, but he stooped a little and moved as if he was unaware of the impression he could make. In contrast, Dave had a lot more personality, though he was less impressive, physically speaking. Paul's suit hung on him as if it had been made for a larger brother. Maybe clothes weren't important to him. In fact, he wouldn't notice anything beyond his realm of interest unless it bit him . . . exactly like Frances, only in a different field . . . another one-track mind. All at once, it hit her that Mick couldn't have had a happy childhood with parents who only focused on themselves.

She glanced sideways at Mick, and the rush of tenderness that shot through her like some hidden fire made her fingertips tingle. It left her a little breathless and reluctant to tear her eyes away. Mick met her gaze. Something must have shown in her face, for his expression softened, and he started to say something, when they were interrupted.

"Mickey! Mick!" Frances' voice floated across the terrace, coming from the house.

Cathy caught a fleeting expression on Paul's face. *So he still cares.* Cathy was surprised.

Mick almost grabbed Cathy's arm, said to his father, "I'll come to see you next week, is that all right?" and, barely waiting for his reply, led her away. But only until he was hidden from his father's sight, then he turned away from the house and went toward the garden again by a roundabout way.

Cathy stopped. "Your mother is in the house."

"I know." Mick's voice was grim. "I have no intention of meeting her. I want to talk to you. Alone."

They turned at the foot of the terrace steps and ran straight into David. "There you are!" He took them both by the arm. "Frances is looking for you."

Cathy felt ready to scream. They joined Frances close to the dancing area. The music was drumming through the room, so she didn't get what Frances asked Mick to do, but it involved him going away, probably to fetch something. She leaned against the wall to wait for his return and watched the dancers. They were a colorful throng. Cathy hummed the tune under her breath and tapped her foot along to the music. She loved to dance. Did Mick dance at all?

Suddenly, a man she had not noticed before asked her if she wanted to dance. Without stopping to think, she agreed. Maybe it would get her mind off the situation, which was getting too complicated to bear.

But when he took her hands, she recognized him. Her heart sank. It was the undesirable cousin who'd been at the bottom of the steps when she'd come down earlier. What was his name? She couldn't remember. Oh yes, Stephen, wasn't it? Angie had described him as a nuisance. Now she couldn't back out anymore. Darn. Couldn't she have opened her eyes before saying yes?

He was a fantastic dancer and gave her the impression she was lithe and light. Cathy started to enjoy herself, when all at once, his hand, which had been on her shoulder, wandered down and stroked her breast.

Cathy shrank away. With clenched teeth, she grabbed his hand and placed it back where it belonged.

Stephen chuckled. "A little prudish, are you?" His hot breath was close to her ear.

"No." Cathy tried to make her voice drip with disdain. "Picky."

All the pleasure of dancing was gone. He tried to pull her closer, but she resisted.

It'll look like a wrestling match in a minute. Cathy tried not to imagine what Frances would say if she saw them.

When he didn't react to her efforts to create more distance, she pinched him hard in the arm.

"Ah . . ." His breath smelled of beer. "A wild cat too?"

Cathy was furious. How could she get rid of him without making a scene in the middle of Frances' party?

"May I take over?" Mick's voice cut through the music.

Stephen gripped Cathy even closer. "No," he said. "Go find yourself another girl . . . or whatever it is you want." He narrowed his eyes to slits and grinned.

"Stephen." Mick's voice was dangerous. "I'll count until three. If you have not unhanded her by then, I'll throw you out."

Stephen loosened his hold a little. "I say, what gives you the right to come up and take her away?"

Cathy pushed him away. "I'm Mick's girl." She whirled around to Mick.

Stephen fell back, his protruding eyes standing out more than ever.

"I told him to get lost, but he didn't pay any attention." She felt humiliated and angry.

Mick took her hand, and they started to dance.

"It's not your fault, Cathy. He's like that. I'm sorry you had to bear him." Mick sighed. "My family is rather tiring at times."

She took a deep breath and managed a shaky smile.

The music changed to a slow tune. "Would you like to continue to dance?" Mick asked.

She nodded. Her heart was beating faster. She was so close to him. And he was so far away. He held her lightly, with the ease that proved a good dancer. Cathy fought hard not to cling too closely to him. It was all she could do if she wanted to keep sane.

But when she lifted her head, she saw Frances standing close by. She watched them with a little frown, as if she was puzzled. "Oh no," Cathy closed her eyes for an instant. "Your mother is watching us."

"This party is getting on my nerves." Mick's voice shook with suppressed violence. "There's much too much family around."

But he drew her a little closer. Suddenly, Cathy did not want to be careful anymore. She would enjoy this night. Tomorrow would take care of itself. She closed her eyes and leaned her cheek against his shoulder. His heart was beating hard, his body warm beside hers. And then, the music closed like a tide over her, and feeling nothing but his arms around her, the rest of the world disappeared without a sound, leaving them in the center, as if they were caught in a bubble of shimmering glass, safe from interruptions and problems. She couldn't prevent a sigh of pure happiness bubbling up from inside. His arms drew her closer. She went with them, sure of herself, as if she knew where she belonged. It felt so right.

When the song changed to a quick rhythm, Mick stopped dancing, but he still held her close. Cathy did not move. She wanted to hold the moment. All around them, people were in motion. Some were leaving the dance floor, others were coming, hustling against them. They stood like an island.

Finally, Cathy lifted her head and leaned back to see him. She smiled at him, trembling deep inside. He bent forward and just when she knew he would kiss her, Angie materialized at their side and tugged at Mick's sleeve.

"Mick!" Her urgent whisper broke the bubble.

Mick closed his eyes and sighed. "What is it now?"

"Let's get off the dance floor first. Quick!"

Mick and Cathy obeyed. He put his arm around her as if it was a perfectly natural thing to do. Cathy kept close by his side. Being in touch with him felt like a well of happiness.

Angie's face was pale. "Dad and Dave are almost at daggers drawn! They're in the living room. I don't know how it started and what it's about, but they're shouting awful things at each other, and a crowd is gathering, and I don't know how to stop them!"

They hurried to the living room. "Where's Frances?" Cathy looked around.

"I don't know." Angie called over her shoulder. "But she won't show up until it's over."

The two men were standing face-to-face. Paul was white like a sheet, whereas Dave's face was beetroot red, his eyes almost unrecognizable. He was shouting at Paul, "She did not marry me for my money! All you can do is talk about words, words, words! No wonder she didn't stay with you! What kind of a man are you?"

Paul lifted his eyebrows. "At least I don't define myself by money."

Mick hurried up to him and put a hand on his shoulder.

Cathy stared at Dave. He was hurt or he would never have blown up like that. Paul must have hit a sore spot. For an instant, she hesitated, then she couldn't bear it anymore. She sidled over to Dave and said in a low voice. "She would never have married you for your money only, Dave. Don't forget she has always had enough choice."

David flashed around to her, his eyes angry. Cathy cringed. She'd said the wrong thing, and now the whole force of the gale was going to be directed at her. Why did she have to jump right in?

From the corner of her eye, she saw Mick nudging his father toward the door.

"Of course not!" David's voice made the chandeliers tingle. "Anybody but this soft-headed professor knows that!"

Paul swung around, but Mick grabbed him by the arm and forced him to go on.

"It's Frances' birthday today." Cathy tried to find words to calm down David. "She wouldn't appreciate that you're fighting with Paul today of all days."

All at once, his anger seemed to evaporate like a cloud. He wiped his eyes with the back of his hand and looked at Cathy with an exhausted expression. "I'm sorry. But he provoked me so much. . . . He said I was . . ." his color was mounting again.

Cathy put a hand on his arm and interrupted him. "Yes, I dare say. But you are married to Frances. He isn't."

Dave frowned at her. Cathy held his eyes. After what seemed like ages, he took a deep breath and nodded. "I see what you mean."

He turned away to leave but something in his face made her say, "Can I join you?"

He glanced down at her, almost back to his old ironic self. "By all means. But you don't need to worry. I won't loose my temper twice in one evening."

Cathy smiled at him. "I was not afraid of that."

His uneven eyebrows lifted. "No? What were you afraid of, then?"

Cathy answered without thinking, "You seemed sad." Then she felt her face going hot. What a thing to say to a grown man after a single day of acquaintance.

But Dave didn't seem to mind. An odd smile hovered around his mouth.

A waiter rushed past them. Cathy saw an opportunity to gloss over her confusion and stopped him. "Could you bring me a glass of white wine, please?" Then she turned to Dave. "Will you take another whiskey?"

He nodded, but there was an element of surprise in his look that left Cathy uneasy. Had it been wrong to ask him? Should she have waited for him to ask her? After all, he was the host. She was running true to form tonight. One goof after another.

When the waiter had brought their glasses, Dave led her out into the garden. All at once, he asked, "You had a job interview yesterday?"

Cathy nodded. She'd rather not think about it again, but it seemed to follow her around like a curse. Maybe Dave wanted to talk about it to take his mind off his outburst.

"What kind of a job was it?" he asked.

Cathy explained as best as she could and was surprised when he listened with genuine interest. His head bent toward her, and he only interrupted her from time to time to ask more questions. She told him a lot more about herself than she had intended, even about the hole in her pantyhose. Finally, he said, his gray eyes smiling, "You know, there's something very British about you, though I gather you spent most of your life over here."

Cathy was surprised. "I know I still have an accent. But otherwise, I shouldn't think . . ." She never told anybody she decided to keep her accent consciously. If she gave it up, or so she had felt in the first horrible months, she would lose a link to her parents. Now, after all those years, it came natural to her.

Dave took her arm and led her back to the terrace. "It's your humor, I believe. A certain understatement. And the ability to make fun of yourself."

"Thank you." Maybe her goofs hadn't been that bad after all.

They entered the large drawing room. Frances stood by the door at the other side of the room. She was the center of a laughing group of people. Little mahogany highlights reflected in her shiny hair. Her face was flushed, her eyes shining. Cathy could well believe that men were standing in line for her.

Cathy glimpsed a free place on a sofa and touched Dave's arm. "I'll sit down for a minute. Thank you for the walk."

He smiled at her. "I thank you." Then he crossed the room with long strides to join Frances.

Cathy collapsed onto the sofa. It was getting late. Her feet hurt, and her eyes were starting to burn. She curled up a little and settled deeper in the cream-colored silk cushion. The talk with David had distracted her, but now the memory of the dance came rushing back. Good thing they had been interrupted. She should never have given in like that. What in the world had possessed her to throw it all overboard and count the world well lost? Was she never going to learn to be on her own? She had to be independent. And not hopelessly in love with Mick . . . who still cared for Nicole, anyway.

She sighed and bent down to massage her ankles. By tomorrow, it would all be over. She would have to continue with her own life, to prove to herself she could make it. All on her own . . . no man next to her. It was all rather difficult.

Somebody sat down on the sofa and made her slide still deeper into the cushions. Cathy looked up. He had short brown hair that stood up like brush. It gave him a boyish appearance. "I saw you break up that fight," he said. "Well done."

Cathy smiled and nodded. Was she supposed to know him? Had Mick presented him to her? She couldn't remember him at all.

"Can I get you a drink?"

Cathy realized her mouth was parched. "Oh yes, please. A lemon punch would be wonderful."

He was back in a short time. "I'm Andrew Hopkins." He handed her the glass.

Good. So she'd not missed anything. "Catherine Albray." Cathy emptied half of her glass in one gulp and felt better.

"It looks as if you and Mick are used to this kind of thing," Andrew said.

"Oh, no!" Cathy shook her head. "It's the first time we had to interfere in a fight."

"You're Mick's girl, aren't you?" Andrew asked.

Cathy avoided his eyes and nodded. If only it were true.

Andrew came a little closer and lowered his voice. "Well, maybe you have some influence over him. He will have told you we've offered him again and again to join Hopkins & Hopkins, but he keeps on refusing. Maybe you could talk to him about it. There are many advantages, you see. A steady income, fewer risks, a big company where he can unfold all his talents best."

Cathy blinked. Mick was a gardener, wasn't he? She'd never heard of a company wooing a gardener.

Andrew winked at her. "It might be a good thing, particularly if one thinks about starting a family."

All at once, Cathy knew she didn't like him. With a frown, she rubbed her left shoulder. "What reasons did Mick give to you when he declined your offer?" She tried not to show her feelings.

Andrew shook his head. "He said he preferred to be his own boss. But that's rather shortsighted of him, I fear."

Cathy emptied her glass and got up. "Well, I don't think I can add anything to that. And, being his girl, I wouldn't discuss it with you even if it were different. Have you ever heard the word loyalty?"

Without giving him time to answer, she stalked to the door and went in search of Mick. At long last, she found him in the kitchen. Kitchens being the center of every party, she was surprised to find he was on his own. Then she took in the gleaming array of stainless steel surfaces and spotless white cupboards and corrected her first impression. It was perfectly natural no one wanted to party in a kitchen so clean it reminded them of a room prepared for open heart surgery.

"Mick!" she felt like running to him, straight into his arms.

He lifted his head. "Yes?"

When he smiled at her like that, she had trouble formulating a coherent question. "What is your job?"

He lifted his eyebrows. "Don't you know? Didn't I tell you?"

Cathy shook her head. "No. I thought you were a gardener."

He grinned. "Kind of. I'm a landscape architect."

An image of swishing grasses leaped to her mind. "So you designed the garden at your house?"

He nodded.

"And the drive up to this house?"

"Yep."

"Why don't you want to work for Hopkins & Hopkins?"

The smile fled from his eyes. "Who told you that?"

"Andrew Hopkins."

Mick's hand clenched. "Don't tell me he had the nerve to approach you?"

Cathy nodded. "He did. Asked me if I was your girl, then enumerated the advantages of working for him and finished with the hint that it would be a lot easier to raise a family with a steady income."

Mick's eyes narrowed. "I don't believe it. What did you answer him?"

Cathy smiled. "I asked him what reasons you had given him for refusing. He said you wanted to be your own boss."

Mick nodded. "That's right. Besides, I don't like him, but I couldn't very well tell him so. And then?"

"Then I said I couldn't add anything to that and asked him if he knew the word loyalty."

Mick stared at her. She could get lost in those lion eyes.

He bent forward to take her hand. "You're a treasure, you know." Cathy's blood ran quicker. She wanted to smooth back his unruly hair, but she was afraid something might break loose that would go beyond her control.

At that moment, Frances appeared behind them. Cathy wanted to stamp her feet like a child.

"There you are!" Frances smiled at them and put her arms around both of them. She seemed to have forgotten their dispute. "Won't you come out to the terrace? It's lovely there."

"Actually, we'd like to say good night, Frances," Mick said.

"But it's early!" Frances pulled back.

Mick raised his eyebrows. "It's three-thirty in the morning."

Frances lifted her hands. "Oh, I know, but it seems just like five minutes since you arrived! Why don't you both stay here for the night? You can have the large guest room."

"No, thank you," Mick answered hastily. "We'd rather go home. You see, we don't see each other all that often."

Cathy swallowed.

"Oh . . . oh, I see." Frances hugged Cathy. A real hug,

not a don't-crumble-my-dress hug. "It was such a wonderful gift that you came to my party, and I'm looking forward to buying your wedding gown with you."

Cathy opened her mouth to protest, but Frances was quicker. "Oh, I know, it'll take some time, but that's fine. Enjoy the rest of the night."

Cathy's heart clenched.

Chapter Seven

"I can't believe we've made it," Cathy said. At long last, they were in the van and left the house behind them.

"It was horrible," he said. "I'm sorry you had to bear my family for so long."

He spoke with so much feeling Cathy wasn't sure if he regretted the whole night. Maybe he'd only gone through the motions whenever the situation demanded a bit more romance. She curled up on her seat, snuggled deeper into her fake-fur-dying-swan jacket and didn't reply. Suddenly, she felt exhausted.

"Tired?" he asked.

"Hmmm."

"We'll be home soon." He accelerated along the empty road. The trees were dark shapes and rushed by like strangers.

Cathy sighed. If only it weren't faked. She would

love to go home with him as if she belonged. Funny that his little house should be so familiar already.

When they arrived, he asked, "Would you like a last drink?"

Cathy nodded. The air had freshened up, and she drew her white jacket closer around her shoulders to protect herself against the breeze coming from the Sound.

They sat down on the porch and stared at the starlit sky without speaking. A cricket chirped in the thick grass, and somewhere, an owl hooted through the night. Cathy could smell a hint of thyme, mixed with dry grass. "It's lovely to be in this quiet world." Cathy kept her voice low so she wouldn't disturb the night. "You know, your mother has a wonderful property, but it cannot hold a candle to this . . ." She hesitated and searched for a word that would fit. "This corner of paradise."

Mick was leaning back in his Adirondack chair, his long legs stretched out in front of him. She could hear the smile in his voice. "Is that how you feel about it?"

Cathy nodded. "Yes. I've never seen a house or a garden that evokes such a . . . a feeling of harmony. It's a gem."

"Nicole wanted to pull it down and build a large bungalow instead." His voice sounded so neutral, it didn't seem to belong to him.

Cathy caught her breath. "Would you have done it?"

He hesitated. "Maybe. I . . . I was pretty besotted at the time."

Cathy didn't know what to reply. The owl hooted again. It seemed to be coming nearer. Mick's voice still sounded detached and strange. "We joked about it, and I said I would have to win the lottery first. She didn't believe me. For some reason, she'd gotten the impression I was rolling in riches."

"It's easy to get that impression when visiting your mother." Cathy tried to sound as calm as he.

He shrugged. "It's Dave's money. And he has three kids of his own. You met them tonight."

"Did I?" Cathy couldn't recall them.

Mick laughed. "Yes, you did."

There was a pause. Something rustled in the bushes close to the porch. A mouse?

Mick continued, "Even the house is more the bank's property than mine. When I told Nicole, she was horrified. Within a week, she had a new lover . . . quite a bit older and so rich, he could pave all the streets in downtown Seattle with gold."

Cathy's throat tightened. "It . . . it must have hurt very much."

He didn't answer, but got up and stared out into the dark garden. "I haven't seen her ever since, until tonight."

Cathy wasn't sure she wanted to hear that.

Mick kept his back to her. "And when she appeared there before me, I suddenly discovered that . . ."

Cathy cringed and balled her hands into fists.

". . . I didn't feel anything anymore."

"What?" Cathy didn't believe her ears. "But why did you put your arm around me and hold me close?" She sat up straight. "I got the impression you wanted to show her you didn't need her anymore, even if the truth was quite different!"

Mick turned on his heels. With two steps, he was beside her, so close she could feel the warmth of his skin.

At that moment, a shrill ringing came from inside the house. "What in the world!" Mick frowned. "Don't they ever leave us in peace?" He didn't move, but listened to the shrill sound of the phone. It didn't stop. "I'm sorry," he finally said. "I have to go and pick it up. I'm expecting a call from a business partner who keeps mixing up the time zones." He smiled at her in a way that made the blood rush to her face. "I'll be back in a minute."

He rushed into the house. Cathy heard him picking up the receiver and could make out his voice, but not the words. She drew up her knees to her chest and hugged them with a sigh. She wasn't sure if she could believe his version of the Nicole story. To her, it hadn't seemed like a love story gone stale. Maybe he just said so in order to please her. Maybe he had seen she was by no means indifferent to him. How humiliating.

His voice came steadily as a faraway sound. It did not sound urgent; he was very calm. No man should be allowed to have a voice like that.

It was an enchanting night; small wonder Mick preferred to sleep outside in summer. She could hear the waves breaking against the cliffs. It was a soothing song. She settled deeper into her chair and rolled into a ball like a kitten. Her eyes closed by their own will. Much better. Maybe they'd stop burning if she kept them closed.

When she woke, sunlight poured into the room. She was lying fully dressed on Mick's bed, snuggled into the quilt. Stretching as far as she could, she remembered the night before. She must have fallen asleep on the Adirondack chair outside. He'd probably found her with her mouth wide open.

With a sigh, she got up. When she took off "Cleopatra's underwear" she felt like Cinderella giving up her ball gown in exchange for the ashes. She'd better get on with it and then out of here as soon as she could, before she embarrassed herself and everybody else involved.

She hurried through a shower, put on her business suit once again and fixed her hair in a coil at the back of her neck. Then she switched on her cell phone, dropped it into her bag, and hastened out to the porch. Mick was sitting on the railing just like the day before. Did he often sit there? She wasn't going to ask. The dream was over.

"Good morning!" She fixed a determined smile on her face.

He jumped up and smiled with those incredible lion eyes she was never going to forget. "Good morning, Cathy."

Her knees felt weak. It wasn't fair to smile like that.

"Would you like a cup of coffee?" he asked.

"Yes." What if it were her life? What if she would always get up and greet the day with him? Wouldn't it be lovely? She added in a flat voice, "I'd very much appreciate if you could drive me to the garage." She glanced at her watch. "I slept so long, they should have my car ready by now."

He seemed puzzled, but did not say anything and went into the house to get the coffee. Cathy followed him with her eyes. All of a sudden, she felt exhausted. When he brought the coffee, she did not sit down to drink it. Forcing a smile, she said between sips of of the scalding hot brew, "So how are we going to break up officially? Do you need me to do anything so it'll be more convincing?"

He looked at her for a minute.

Her throat started to hurt. To get it over with, she rushed on, "Maybe it's best if we say we don't suit each other. Though your mother doesn't agree." Funny, how every word seemed to saw a piece out of her soul. Pressing her lips together, she forced herself to go on. "We could say now that we had some time together, we found it did not work."

"I don't agree," Mick said.

"No?" For a fleeting moment, Cathy met his eyes and averted her gaze immediately. How could he smile like that when she was fighting to be sensible?

"Well," she swallowed, ". . . we might also say it's nobody's business and refuse to answer all questions."

"You got me wrong," Mick said. "It's not that I don't agree with the way of breaking up, but with the breaking up itself."

Cathy caught her breath. Her heart beat like a drum, filling all her aching inside.

Mick took her hands. There was something compelling about the way he held her . . . firm, yet without using any force. He had held her like that, lightly, from the beginning; Cathy would have recognized his touch with bound eyes. She wished he would never let her go.

His eyes searched her face. "I've been trying to tell you since last night. When I saw Nicole, I realized she doesn't mean anything to me anymore." He paused. "That was one thing I had not expected. The other was that I should fall for a small woman with a lovable snub-nose, freckles, and a passion for honesty."

A lump stuck in her throat and made it hard to breathe.

"But I have." Mick's smile deepened, the orange flecks in his eyes very much in evidence. "And I will resist all efforts to remove you from my life again." He searched her face, his eyes suddenly anxious. "Unless you'd prefer me not to?"

Cathy opened her mouth, but no sound came out.

Mick drew her close to him. "Cathy, there were times yesterday when I felt we really belonged together, no make-believe. Like when we danced." He hesitated. His eyes searched hers. "But then, I wasn't sure. You . . . you seemed very far away and . . . and determined to stay there."

Cathy didn't know how to reply. She stared down at a button on his shirt, then up again. Swallowing hard, she tried to sort out the jumbled feelings fighting inside her. But when she opened her mouth, a loud ringing interrupted them.

Cathy jumped. "That's my mobile phone!" She ran past him and looked for her handbag. Where had she left it? She finally found it in the living room, fished out her phone and checked the display. Dan's number. Cathy frowned. He never called during the day, unless it was something urgent.

She pressed the green button. "Hi, Dan." Her voice sounded flat.

"Cathy! Thank God I finally reach you! Where are you?"

Cathy cringed. She knew every little nuance of his voice. Dan was in a white hot rage.

"Why . . . I told you . . ." she tried to prevaricate. "I called last night . . ."

"I know you did," he said. "I even believed you stayed with that stupid friend of yours. But this morning, the insurance company called and wanted to know some more details about an accident that was supposed to have taken place the day before yesterday in Seattle."

Cathy closed her eyes. "Oh, no." She dropped into one of the chairs in front of the empty fireplace. Mick came in, threw her a glance and froze. Dan's words came as an audible, if tinny, diatribe over the phone.

"I told them it was all a big mistake, but they put me on to a police station who confirmed the whole thing. They guy at the police acted as if you were a lost criminal. They could even tell me where they put the damaged car. So I called them and they confirmed it's yours! I'm crazy with worry. Where are you? Nobody could tell me that. And why were you in Seattle in the first place? I'm worried out of my mind."

Helpless, Cathy looked at Mick. "I'm still in Seattle." She had to force herself to answer.

"So it is true!"

Cathy held the phone away from her ear.

Dan's voice exploded into the room. "I don't believe this! Why did you lie to me?"

Cathy's stomach lumped up. "I . . . I'll explain it all, Dan." Her voice sounded small. "But I can't do it on the phone. I'll come home today; my car has been repaired. I . . . I promise I'll explain it all."

Mick turned on his heels and went to the front door, but Cathy held him back with a wave of her hand. She needed him.

"You don't have to come home!" Dan's voice was grim.

"Why, what do you mean?" Cathy's hand shook, clamped on the phone.

"I'm in Seattle."

"You're what?" Cathy jumped up.

"I took a plane right after the call from the garage."

"But that wasn't necessary!"

"How on earth should I have known?" Dan shouted

so loud, it filled the small room. "All I knew was your car was wrecked and you had disappeared."

"I haven't disappeared." Cathy clenched her teeth.

"If you tell me you are with that impossible Mary-Lou and secretly go somewhere else where I can't find you, I call that disappearing!"

"Oh no, Dan, I never meant—"

"Where are you?" He almost deafened her.

Cathy threw a wild look at Mick. "I . . . I'm with a friend."

"You don't have any friends in Seattle."

"Listen, Dan." Cathy rubbed her shoulder. "Why don't you come here? We could talk, I'll explain it all quietly, and then we'll return home together."

Dan sighed. "Oh, all right. What's the address?"

Cathy stared at Mick, her eyes wide. With two long strides, he reached the high table that separated the kitchen from the living room and grabbed from it a letter with his address on top. It was an old electricity bill. She spelled it out for Dan, then hung up and fell back into her chair. With a sigh, she passed her hands over her face. For a moment, neither said a word. Then Mick sat down opposite her and bent forward, his elbows on his knees. "Cathy." His voice forced her to lift her head. His eyes looked troubled. "Who's Dan?"

Cathy made a wry mouth. "My brother."

His face cleared. "Your brother! I thought it was . . ." He stopped himself.

She supplied the words for him. "My lover?"

He nodded, then pushed back his hair, which had

flopped forward into his face. "I know it's none of my business, but won't you tell me why it's such a secret you are in Seattle?"

Embarrassed, Cathy took a cushion that pressed against her back and placed it on her knees. She stared at it as if it held the answer to all the problems in the world. Taking a corner of the faded red material between her fingers, she said, "I need to be free."

Mick frowned. "I don't understand."

Cathy sighed and let the corner of the cushion glide through her fingers. It felt like velvet, but looked like faded cotton. Searching for the right words, she started in a low voice, "I've been wanting to tell you. I . . . I hope you'll understand." For an instant, she met his lion eyes, then looked at the cushion again. She took the corner and made it slide through her fingers. "Dan is three years older than I am. When . . . when my parents died, he pretty much took their place."

"I thought you'd gone to live with your uncle?" Mick's voice sounded soft.

Cathy nodded. "Yes. But he's a professor." She shrugged. "Words are more important to him than children. And Chrystal—that's my aunt—is an artist. Eccentric and colorful, but not someone to snuggle up with when you're lonely." Her eyes met his for a fleeting moment, then she added hastily, "Don't get me wrong. They're great people . . . but they were unaccustomed to children. It took us a long time to get a bit closer."

Mick nodded without interrupting her. Cathy was grateful for that.

"But Dan was there for me. He protected me and helped me with everything. My big brother . . . I was so proud to have him."

She stared at Mick, willing him to understand. "You see, he took over as father and mother. He checked my homework. Practiced softball with me. Once, he even helped me dye my hair." A wry smile tweaked a corner of her mouth. "He comforted me when my first boyfriend dumped me. When he got his driving license, he drove me everywhere. Later, he taught me how to drive. He taught me virtually everything."

She smoothed the cushion on her knees without seeing it. "When I finished school, I moved into the house he had already bought, and we both thought it was great. He . . . he didn't want to control me, but of course he couldn't help knowing all my friends. And when he doesn't approve, he can't hold back." She twirled the red corner around her finger and let it go again.

She sighed. "So we have fights. He keeps telling me how to improve my position in the company. How to dress. How to do this. How to do that. At first, I was grateful for advice, but somehow, I changed with time and don't want to be told what to do all the time, even if I don't always get it right and now . . ." She left the sentence trailing and suddenly lifted her head. "I'm twenty-six. I need to stand on my own feet. Only it would hurt him so much if he knew I was planning to move out. It would lead to endless discussions. He wouldn't have a quiet minute, worrying himself crazy."

She looked at Mick. "I dread that."

Mick cleared his throat. "I understand."

Cathy lifted one corner of her mouth in a halfhearted smile. "I know you do," she said. "You've got more or less the same problem with Frances."

"Yes."

Cathy felt better. "One day, I read the job offer of the Convention Center by chance and applied without telling Dan." She stared down at the cushion and twisted the soft corner into a roll. "I felt like a secret agent or something. And . . . and deceitful." She met the lion eyes defiantly. "You may have noticed I'm not good at hiding things."

"I noticed." He smiled, his dimple showing.

Cathy swallowed. "When the Convention Center invited me, I couldn't believe my luck, but at first I didn't know how to organize it so Dan wouldn't realize what was going on. I . . . I didn't want him to know anything until it was all tied up. In the end, I told him I would spend the day with Mary-Lou, a colleague he doesn't approve of." She grinned. "I knew he would never call her."

"And then you hit my van." He moved forward to sit on the armrest of her chair.

"Yes." She released the much suffering cushion. For some reason, she was suddenly shy and dared not meet his eyes.

"Cathy." He took her hands and pulled her close to him. "Don't you think . . . ?"

A strangled sound from the open door made them jump apart.

"You must be Dan." Mick got up. "Nice to meet you."

Standing next to Mick, Dan seemed small, though he was of average height. By the breadth of his shoulders, you could tell he used to play football. His face had the same shape as Cathy's, making an uncanny resemblance, but his eyes were a startling indigo blue and his hair darker than hers. He looked like someone who knew himself and his world, confident of his place and his abilities, though it was obvious by the way he opened and closed his hands he was out of his depth at the moment.

He shook hands with Mick without once taking his eyes off his sister. Cathy jumped up and stood in front of her chair. She had a queasy feeling deep in her stomach. Dan hugged her as if in spite of himself. Fierce and short, the embrace shook Cathy even more than his voice. It was so rough, she almost didn't recognize it. "Thank God you're okay. I had the most horrible visions."

"I'm sorry." Cathy swallowed.

"Why are you in Seattle? Why didn't you tell me? Why didn't you tell me you have a boyfriend?"

Cathy lifted both hands. "No, no, you got that wrong. I'm not Mick's . . ."

"Hellooo . . ." A voice came from the open front door. "Anybody home?"

Frances appeared in the doorway, followed by Angie.

"Oh, Cathy, you're still here! How nice!" Frances floated across the threshold. "We dropped in with the hope of seeing you, because I wanted to tell you how much everybody liked you at the party yesterday!"

Mick stepped behind his mother's back and made frantic signs at Angie, who stared from a puzzled Dan to the frozen Cathy.

When Frances opened her mouth, Mick interrupted her. "Frances, this is Dan Albray, Cathy's brother."

Frances rounded on Dan. "Oh, how nice! I never knew Cathy had a brother!" She took the hand he offered with enthusiasm. "You look very much like each other! Why didn't you come to the party too? I'd have been delighted."

An expression of utter bewilderment passed over Dan's face. "The party?" he repeated as if he didn't know such a thing existed.

"Why, yes, my birthday party yesterday!" Frances turned to her son. "Mick, be a darling, and get me something cold to drink, will you? The heat is killing me!"

"I'll get it." Angie retreated to the kitchen area.

Cathy opened her mouth to say something, but Frances beat her to it with a smile, "My dear, you know, I have seen the most wonderful gown for you! When I woke up this morning, I remembered I had seen it somewhere, and I dug out a pile of magazines and after hours and hours, I found it! It's delightful, with a large hoop and . . ."

Dan blanched. He wheeled to Cathy with eyes that seemed to burn into her. "Gown?" His voice sounded hoarse. "You're engaged?"

Cathy threw a wild glance at Mick. Angie started forward, a glass in her hand, and said, "Yes, but . . ."

"No," Mick interrupted her, his voice in odd contrast to the tension in the room. "Cathy is not engaged to me."

"What?" Frances stared at him. "But you said yesterday you . . ."

"I know we did." Mick shook his head. "But it's not true."

All at once, Frances looked her age. She passed a hand over her face.

Cathy couldn't stand to see her like that. Without stopping to think, she jumped forward and put a hand on her arm. "No, no it's not as you think, Frances!"

Dan stood rooted to the ground.

Mick turned to Cathy. "So we're engaged?" His eyebrows rose. The dimple in his left cheek deepened. "I'll hold you to that."

Cathy caught her breath. "But . . ."

"Are you engaged or aren't you?" Dan found his voice.

Cathy knew that voice. Speechless, she stared into her brother's eyes, and all of a sudden, she knew she had to confess it all.

"Frances," she said. "Would you very much mind if I took a turn about the garden with Dan? He has only just arrived, and I need to discuss some family business with him."

"But I do mind!" Frances waved the glass which Angie had handed her. "I'm at a loss. I have certainly lived my life to the fullest, but I am thankful to say I always knew whether I was engaged or not!"

Cathy closed her eyes. She would have preferred to have it out just between herself and Dan.

Mick faced his mother. "It was a lie." His voice sounded grim.

"But no!" Angie jumped up from the seat she had fallen into. "You can't say that!"

"Yes, I can." Mick faced his mother. "You were convinced I was gay, and there was no way to get that crazy idea out of your mind."

Angie fell back into her seat and covered her face with her hands. Dan stared at Mick, open-mouthed.

Frances opened her beautiful eyes wide. "But Mickey, I know now I was mistaken. You've got Cathy and . . ."

"That's just it," Mick said with a tired movement of his hands. "I don't have Cathy. We made it up."

Dan gulped. Frances' head swiveled toward Cathy, then back to Mick. "You what?"

"We made it up," Mick repeated, determined now. "I met Cathy by accident, and when you saw us at the Italian restaurant, you absolutely wanted to take her for . . ." He hesitated.

"But isn't she the girl you met via the Internet?" Frances interrupted.

"No."

"Well!" All of a sudden, Frances beamed at him. "Here I'm worried to death, and in fact, you don't have one girl, but several. That's great!"

Mick winced. "It's not true!"

Frances jumped up and made a large movement with her arms. "Now that's enough arguing to and fro. In fact, it's all very simple." She pointed at Cathy. "Cathy, are you in love with Mick?"

Cathy recoiled. "I . . . I'm . . ."

Satisfied, Frances nodded "I thought so." Then she faced her son, "Mick, are you in love with Cathy?"

Mick started to laugh. "Really, you're too much, Frances."

Frances grinned. "Oh, I understand, you prefer to discuss it between yourselves, with a romantic sunset or something. Well, I don't care how you ever got to know each other, but I know one thing. You are made for each other; so that's perfect."

Cathy's mouth dropped open.

Frances continued with a smile that lightened up her beautiful face, "And whether you're engaged or not doesn't matter; you'll clear up this misunderstanding soon enough!" She finished her glass and put it down on the table. In one fluid movement, she stood up and turned to Dan, offering him her hand with a regal move. "It was nice to get to know you. I hope you'll move to Seattle too, since Cathy is already planning to come."

Cathy swallowed.

Dan's head shot up. The expression in his eyes made her wince. "You're moving to Seattle?"

Cathy took all her courage in her hands. "I applied for a job."

Dan seemed to want to ask something else, but stopped with a glance at Frances.

Cathy's heart ached. She bit her lip. Should she go

up to him or keep at a distance? A distance she had wanted, after all. If only it didn't hurt so much.

"All right, I hope I'll see you again soon!" Frances had not noticed Dan's reaction. She bent forward and breathed a kiss onto Cathy's cheek, patted Mick's cheek, took Angie by the arm and dragged her through the door.

Chapter Eight

All at once, the room seemed empty. They heard the car doors bang. Then the motor started, and the sound of the driving car died away. Cathy heard her own breathing. She was aware of Mick standing beside her without moving. Suddenly, Mick said, "I've got to see to something in the garden."

As his steps faded away, Dan asked, his voice hard, "Why couldn't you tell me you wanted to move to Seattle?"

"I . . . I needed to do something all by myself." If only her answer didn't sound so threadbare.

"Why do you want to go away?"

It was torture. And she had started it. "Because . . . because I need to stand on my own feet . . . ." She looked away.

Silence filled the room. "I never meant to boss you around." Dan stared at her with a scowl.

"I know." Her voice did not seem to belong to her. He looked puzzled and irritated at the same time.

"I meant it for the best."

She grit her teeth. "Yes. I'm aware of that."

He grabbed her arm. Suppressed fury, concern, and the relief of tension after having found her were written large across his face. He almost spat out the next sentence. "So why on earth do you think it's necessary to slink away and get a job miles away from home?"

Her stomach coiled itself up, like a heavy animal. This was the situation she had dreaded and had tried to avoid at all cost. To face him with nothing but a total loss, to have to admit she was unable to manage on her own, oh, how she had hoped to prove the opposite.

In her dreams, she took him on a surprise trip, showed him her new job contract with a much better salary than her present one, and then she presented him her new, just-rented apartment, with a view of Elliott bay, sparkling in sunlight . . . .

Instead, she had wrecked her car, lost all chances on the job, and had fallen in love instead of being in control and mature and . . . She stopped herself by saying, "I . . . I needed to prove to myself I can manage on my own."

Dan's left eye narrowed. Oh, how she hated that. Whenever she told him about her dreams, her crazy ideas, he put on his disdaining expression. The result was always the same: She dropped her dreams like hot potatoes. But not again. Today, she would stand her ground.

"Dan, I'm truly sorry, and I don't want to hurt you at all. But please leave me alone."

He jumped up and nodded. "All right. Suit yourself."

Without another word, he turned on his heels and stalked off, out of the house, and down the drive. Cathy stared at his back. It was fury impersonated. Suddenly, something in her broke, and she ran after him.

"Dan!"

He veered around. "What?" His eyes were cold.

Breathless, she said, "Don't go like that. Please. Why don't you stay and . . . and drink a cup of coffee. Then we'll discuss it quietly. There's no need to be like that."

His mouth was one firm line. "You just told me to leave you alone."

Cathy cringed. "Yeah, but I didn't mean it like that. I only meant that I . . . that I . . ." She struggled to find the right words.

"That you don't need me anymore."

"No!" She couldn't bear the hidden sadness in his voice. "It's hard to explain. Won't you stay . . . ?"

Dan shook his head. "No. It's noon already. I don't want to return to Spokane late at night. Come along now."

Cathy recoiled. She couldn't go. She had to talk to Mick. She had to explain to him how she felt. She . . .

"I don't see any reason for you to linger on. It's still a long drive home, and from what I gathered you had a long night yesterday. It would be only sensible to leave now."

"No, I can't." Cathy turned to stare at the little house. Mick was nowhere to be seen.

"How did you plan to get home anyway? Or did you not plan anything at all?"

His sarcasm hit her as if it were a physical blow. "I was just on my way to collect my car," she said with all the dignity she could muster.

"Good. I'll drive you to the garage, then I'll return my rented car, and afterward, we can go home together."

Cathy's heart sank. It sounded so sensible. Darn. It was always like that. Whatever he said, it sounded as if it were the only logical thing to do. She swallowed. "I . . . I believe Mick wanted to drive me to the garage."

Dan narrowed his left eye. "He's not going to feel deprived if he can save that trip, will he? Besides, it's perfect. I can save the flight back, and you don't need to drive home on your own."

Cathy once again turned around and scanned the ground for Mick. Darn. Where was he? "I'll just go inside and ask him."

"But please be quick about it. I meant it when I said I want to get started soon."

Cathy ran to the house. She found Mick in the little kitchen, peering into the fridge.

"Mick!"

He looked up, a smile on his lips. Then he met her eyes. His smile fled. "What happened?"

"Dan . . . Dan wants to drive home now. And he wants me to go with him!"

His face went blank. "Yes?"

"I . . . I believe it makes sense," Cathy said, though something inside her protested with vehemence.

Mick didn't reply. He stood like a statue.

Breathless, Cathy continued, "Dan wants to drive me to the garage, and then we can go home together. It will save him the flight back, and I don't have to drive on my own."

Mick swallowed, but when he opened his mouth, Dan appeared at the door. "Cathy, are you ready? We have to go."

Cathy whipped around. "I'm coming." She hurried across the room and grabbed her handbag. There was nothing else to pack.

Dan stood at the door and tapped his foot.

Cathy hesitated, then dashed up to Mick, stood on tiptoe and kissed his cheek. "Thank you. Thank you so much."

He bent his head, then lifted his hand as if to hold her. But halfway up, he stopped dead. His arm dropped to his side.

She was already at the door, when he said, "Wait." His voice sounded rough.

Cathy stopped.

"You don't have the address of the garage."

She felt her face going red. Of course she'd forgotten the most elementary thing.

Dan threw her an exasperated glance and brushed past her into the house. "It's better if you give it to me."

Cathy felt tears welling up inside her.

Mick scribbled something onto the back of an old envelope, dodged Dan's outstretched hand and held it out to Cathy.

Startled, she tried to read his face, but for once, she couldn't penetrate his barriers. The lion eyes looked aloof, not admitting her.

"Have a good trip" was all he said when she took the piece of paper with a shaking hand.

The air conditioner fought against the temperature inside her car and managed to cool it down one degree at a time. The motor hummed as if there had never been an accident. Dan had taken the driver's seat without asking. She threw a sidelong glance at him. The muscles around his mouth were tense. Oh yes, he was still angry, though it wouldn't show in his tempered driving. His iron self-control never snapped.

Was she afraid of him? No. She knew he would never lay a hand on her, though his muscles could intimidate. No, she was afraid of losing him altogether. Of hurting him, her one and only real family. If only she could make him understand. "Dan," she said in a low voice.

He didn't reply. Maybe he hadn't heard her. Maybe it wasn't a good time to spring it at him. There was a fuming lorry before them, creeping down Interstate 5 with the speed of a turtle. The traffic was crushing. Soon now, they would reach the exit for Interstate 90, going east. Cathy sighed. She'd been filled with hope when she had come that way. Life had been so exciting. A challenge. A promise. But it was over now. Out of her window she could catch glimpses of Mount Rainier, standing like a picture postcard in the brilliant sunlight. It had greeted her like an old friend when she had first seen it. Now she had to go. Crushed. Defeated. A loser. What had she gained? A torn pantyhose, an immense bill for the repair of her car, and—worst of all—a brother she had hurt. With fierce concentration, she avoided thinking of Mick.

She stole another glance at Dan. He might have been alone in the car, for all the notice he took of her.

A row of road signs, perched high across the street, crept closer. The sunlight played on the green background with the white letters. Cathy's eyes focused on the red and blue emblem at the side announcing the beginning of I-90. It looked like a crest of arms. Her road to dreams. It had not held the promises she had expected.

Following the curve of the road, they merged inch by inch into I-90, head-to-head with three other lanes of tightly packed cars. Here, traffic finally loosened up. Dan sighed with relief and put his foot down on the accelerator.

They thundered into Mount Baker tunnel. Cathy closed her eyes. She felt wrung out like a dish cloth.

The sound of the wheels changed. They didn't whine anymore, they droned. Cathy knew without opening her eyes they were crossing Lake Washington on the floating bridges.

All of a sudden, he said, "Who's this Mick?"

Cathy jumped. Her eyes flew open, and she was almost blinded by the sun reflecting off the water. "He . . . he's a landscape architect."

"I don't care what he does." Dan threw her an irritated glance. "You don't need to tell me either he lives in a small house and has a battered van because I've seen it. What I really want to know—"

Cathy felt a wave of irritation. "If his van is battered, it's due to me."

Dan's eyebrows drew together. "What's that?"

"On my way to the job interview, I happened to bump his van slightly," Cathy said. "That's how we met."

He saw through her story, as always. "The damage to your car did not happen with a simple bump."

She did not reply. Anything she said now would only make it worse.

He waited for a while, but when it became apparent she was not going to answer, he said, "How come you went to that birthday party of his mother's? And what's this about being engaged? You've only known the fellow for two days!"

Cathy swallowed. How could she explain? "I . . . I met his mother, and she invited me to her party. Since I had to wait for the repair of the car anyway, it was perfect." She fell silent.

"And the engagement?"

Cathy stared out of the window. They were approaching Mercer Island now. Green trees around the shore gave it a lush, even luxurious appearance. The road ahead was rising, climbing onto the island like a fat alligator, its long tail hanging into the sea. Soon they would ride on its back, straight across the northern tip of the island, then over the remaining arm of Lake Washington. And every mile took her farther away. "I'm not engaged." The words hurt in her throat.

Dan shook his head. "Don't tell me there's nothing between you because I'm not going to believe it. I've never seen you look at a guy like that."

Cathy linked her hands in her lap and pressed them together until they hurt.

"Cathy." Dan's voice changed, it was gentle now. "I believe I understand how you feel. But it won't do. Believe me."

Something heavy lodged on her chest and refused to go. "Why not?" Her throat hurt.

He hesitated. "It's hard to say. But I know you. From what I've seen of him, it would never work out."

Every word was like a stab of a knife, turning with a twist inside her wound. "I don't believe that."

He threw her an exasperated glance, his blue eyes blazing. "All right then, since you want it. The guy's a softy. And he may be gay, for all I know."

Her fury surprised her. She almost jumped out of her seat. "He's not gay!"

Dan lifted one hand. "Hey, keep your hair on. I didn't say he was. But his mother thought so, and from what I know, the last person to accept that kind of thing is a mother."

"His mother takes all kinds of strange notions into her head, at regular intervals." Her voice sounded like ice. "If you knew her, you wouldn't believe a word."

He shrugged. "As you say. But I still don't believe that guy is right for you."

Cathy wanted to strangle him. "If being a softy means he considers the feelings of others and does not act like a macho, then a softy is the very man for me!"

Dan curled his lips.

Cathy saw it and blew her stack. For a moment, all she could see was red-hot color blinding her, then it left, leaving her foaming with rage. "You are the most arrogant, conceited man I know! You order me around, you control my friends, my job, my life. Whatever I do, it isn't good enough. You treat me as if I were a child, all in front of others!" She knew she was close to tears and added the crowning insult with a trembling voice. "You don't even let me make scrambled eggs because I burned them once ages ago!"

She could see he was startled. It was the first time she had attacked him like that, losing control completely.

He rallied quickly enough, though. "You have to admit I'm good at making scrambled eggs."

Her sense of humor got the better of her. Could it be they were fighting over scrambled eggs, of all the things in the world?

She shook her head. Her anger evaporated. "Yes," she sighed. "I know. All I'm saying is I might be able to do it just as well if you had given me the slightest chance to learn."

"Cathy," he spoke as if she were dimwitted. "May I remind you that you never wanted to learn? You were quite happy to leave it all to me."

He checked the rearview mirror and pulled out of the lane to overtake a gray pickup truck.

To grant him justice, she had to admit he was right.

"So I've changed." She sounded sullen, even to her own ears.

She knew he narrowed his left eye, even though she could not see it. "But it's not fair to blame me just because you changed, isn't it?"

Oh, blast it, he was at it again. His irrefutable logic chewed her fragile arguments to shreds. She refused to answer and turned her back on him, staring out of the window. They were crossing the eastern area of King County now. With blind eyes, Cathy stared into the thick forest on her side. Like a dim memory, she remembered her pleasure two days earlier to see a wilderness immediately next to a town as overwhelming in size as Seattle. Before coming up, she'd read something about the "Mountains to Sound Greenway Trust" that made this stretch of paradise next to the roaring highway possible, and it had intrigued her and delighted her . . . but right now, she couldn't care less.

"Cathy." Dan still spoke with that patient voice. "You will at least admit I know you better than anyone else, don't I?"

In spite of herself, she nodded, refusing to take her eyes off the forest.

"So why don't you trust me if I say the guy is wrong for you?"

She pressed her lips together. *Because I feel it.* Loudly, she said, "Frances said we were perfect for each other."

"But you just told me yourself no one should believe a word Frances says."

Cathy felt like screaming. She was never, ever, going

to get the better of him. "I'm going to sleep." She pulled up her legs and curled together in her seat.

Although she tried to sleep, it did not come. Her eyes were burning, and she kept them closed, but the images of the last few days haunted her. Mick's lion eyes smiling at her. His arm around her shoulder when they had the picture taken. The skyline of Seattle by night. The gentle swinging of the grasses in Mick's garden. She longed for him so fiercely it hurt.

From time to time, she squinted at the scenery. Lake Sammamish glistened on her left, then was gone. The road rose steadily through the Cascade Range toward Snoqualmie Pass, bare rock breaking through the soil. Dark fir trees lined the highway, like brooding sentinels, making sure she did not break out and run back to where she wanted to be.

At some point, she must haven fallen asleep after all. When she woke, they were just rushing past the exit toward Moses Lake.

Good. They were almost home. Cathy stretched her cramped legs as best as she could.

Dan smiled at her. "Feeling better now?"

She nodded.

"I stopped on the way and bought a drink, but you were dead to the world." He made a move of his head toward the back of the car. "But I got you some water and put it on the backseat, only I'm afraid it fell off in the meantime. They had run out of still water, so I took the least sparkling one."

"Thanks." Cathy turned around and fished the bottle

out of the dark recess behind his seat. This was the nice side of his character. He would never forget to care for you. You were under his wing, well protected, and once there you could come to no harm. It was a safe and cozy position. Unless you tried to fly by yourself.

Neither said anything for a long time. All of a sudden, Dan broke the silence. "You know, there's something I don't understand."

Cathy braced herself. "Well?"

"Why are you so set on that Mick guy if you want to be independent? The way it seems to me, you think you've found someone better, so you chuck the old one away."

The bitterness in his voice caught her heart. "No! Oh no, Dan, that's not true! Please believe me." She searched his face. It might as well have been carved of stone. He stared straight ahead.

She laid a hand on his leg. "Dan, the one has nothing at all to do with the other. I wanted to be more independent, that's true, but it has nothing to do with Mick. Nothing. I applied for that job because I thought it would be a good thing for me, to get ahead." She swallowed, then added, "I do believe it makes sense for us to separate a bit more. Mick never entered the picture at all. Why, I didn't know him until two days ago."

He stared straight ahead as if the long ribbon of the highway in front of him held all the attractions in the world. "Well, whatever you wanted, you were quick in finding yourself another man to lean on."

Her hand fell away. He was right. Oh, how right he was. She couldn't start a new relationship the minute she told Dan to leave her alone. She had sensed it all along, but whenever she was close to Mick, all her sensible arguments failed her, and she just reveled in his presence. She couldn't see him again. It would erode all she tried to build up.

She stared straight ahead. Every now and then, a dark red barn would show against the dazzling blue sky, but otherwise, the world was filled with acres and acres of farmland. The fields undulated in soft curves as if a gentle hand from above had smoothed out any irregularities. Most of the crop was already cut down, leaving just the golden stubble, with the reddish brown earth showing underneath. Huge bales of straw were dotted over the fields in regular intervals, like giant balls to play with. They stretched as far as the horizon, where they balanced on the edge of the world like objects of art. As a child, Cathy had often wondered what would happen if you could lift the corner of a field as if it were a blanket. They'd all start to roll. What a sight it would be.

She smiled a little at herself. It had been easier then. Of course, she'd been lonely, and the States had terrified her at the beginning. It was all so different from England. But at least she didn't have to fight against herself. Now she was so afraid she would end up on her nose . . . just as Dan has predicted. "I don't wish to lean on anybody at all," she said. "I'll make it on my own." She felt his gaze, blue and cold, and met it defiantly. "I swear it."

Chapter Nine

Cathy sat with crossed legs on her bed, the telephone in front of her. In her hands, she held the envelope Mick had given her. It was the only thing she had to show for her two days in Seattle. She stared at his handwriting on the envelope. It was a scrawl, barely legible. She followed his writing with the tip of her finger, then put the envelope up to her nose and smelled it, searching in vain for a trace of him.

The door banged. She heard Dan's steps coming in. With a quick move, she stuffed the envelope behind her back, feeling the blood rush up to her face. If he caught her! . . . She'd die of mortification.

But his steps started to make a different sound, clicked louder. He'd gone into the tiled kitchen. Cathy sighed. Things had changed a lot since their return. He was as considerate as ever, friendly too, but there was a strained note in everything he did, and the old companionship was gone. A week ago, he would have come to her room and asked her how her day had been. Nowadays, he never did that, as if her room was forbidden territory. She'd often wished to have a room all to herself, where she wouldn't be disturbed, but she had never imagined it to be like that . . . as if she were a leper.

With a sigh, she put the precious envelope in her drawer and forced herself to join him in the kitchen. "Hi, Dan."

"Cathy." He barely glanced at her. "I'm going out again in a minute, I just wanted to grab a bite and take a shower."

"Fine." This had changed as well. He used to tell her where he went, and who he met. Now he told her he would be gone . . . and he was away from home more often than not. She'd never felt so lonely in her life.

When Dan had left, she returned to sit on her bed and stared at the telephone again. On the other side of the envelope, she had found Mick's address, and with the help of a directory, she had dug out his telephone number. Now she knew it by heart.

And never dialed it.

Tonight, the temptation was almost irresistible.

If she could hear his whiskey voice, she'd feel a lot better. Spokane was getting on her nerves. So staid. So slow. So predictable. Nothing like Seattle. She missed the sea, with its promise of freedom, of faraway shores where dreams could come true and miracles would happen.

She eyed the telephone.

It would feel so good to hear his voice and that hidden smile deep down. Why not call him and ask if the repair of the van had been expensive? It would only be polite.

A nasty little voice inside her protested, *Yeah, and then you'd drop into his arms like a ripe plum, and . . . exit your precious independence. Just like Dan said.*

Rubbish, her other voice protested. *It won't do any harm. Besides, I can't fall into his arms if he's several hundred miles away. He might just as well be in Africa.*

Oh, no, the derisive voice inside her laughed like a goat. *You'd manage it even at long distance. Then where would you be?*

Cathy sighed. She picked up the telephone and tapped in his number without touching the digits.

It would be so easy. She could just be friends with him, couldn't she?

No, you can't, the nasty voice replied. *He made it clear he would like to be more than just a friend, and you have as much resolve as a jelly fish. You would topple right over.*

Disgusted with herself, Cathy threw the telephone onto her bed again.

All right, if she had to be independent, she'd better stop losing time.

She rushed to the living room and switched on the computer she shared with Dan. With a humming sound, it awoke to life.

Cathy tapped her fingers while the computer took

its time to identify who it was and where to find what it knew.

Once on the Internet, it took her only a few seconds to hit the recruitment pages of *The Seattle Times*. She'd been there before.

She entered a selection—a very broad one—and started to read. A scowl gathered on her forehead.

Talented. She snorted. Of course. That was just one of the many words to describe her.

Motivated. Okay, that might work out. She was motivated enough.

Excellent presentation skills. No. Not really.

Dynamic. Shaking her head, she clicked on.

Commitment to excellence. Well!

Able to make quick decisions. She could still hear Mick's voice, amused, above the roar of the traffic. "You're good at making quick decisions, aren't you?"

With clenched teeth, she read on.

Proven track record. She'd proven nothing yet. Not to herself, even less to others.

Exceptional interpersonal skills. Yeah, she was good at that. She even almost got along with her brother.

Disgusted, Cathy pushed the keyboard away. A headache started to pucker behind her lids.

It was no use at all.

She couldn't apply for anything.

She had the self-confidence of a field mouse tonight.

Turning a streak of hair around her finger, she stared into space. No way could she compose a cover letter bristling with assertiveness.

Not tonight.

Not tomorrow.

Maybe never.

Maybe she should call Mick, to ask him about field mice in general and in particular.

She bit her lip and blinked hard. Pulling herself together, she made it back to her room to collect the telephone.

Back in the kitchen, she placed it on the table as if it were fragile. The room smelled of lemon washing liquid.

Dusk had fallen and made the room dark and oppressive. Cathy switched on the light. The little red lamp she loved offered no comfort tonight.

She sighed and opened the fridge. It stared back at her with yawning eyes. There was a piece of cheese, yellow at the edges, two slices of toast, and pickled onions. True riches. In the farthest corner, she found a yogurt.

Vanilla.

Not her favorite flavor, but it would have to do. The ones with orange flavor were all long gone.

Turning it to the light, she checked the due date. Yesterday. Yuk. Then she shrugged. Oh well, it usually kept longer than that.

She put the yogurt down on the gleaming white kitchen table, then pulled out a chair and fell into it.

She didn't even need to glance down once to open the lid.

As she licked off the aluminum foil, Cathy concentrated on the telephone and tried to hypnotize it.

"Come on, ring."

The telephone did not react. It sat there, in the discreet anthracite color Dan had chosen, and refused to communicate.

"Ring. That's your job." Cathy pressed her lips together. "If you don't ring, I don't need you."

She stirred the yogurt as if she wanted to whip up cream, without taking her eyes off the phone. "You know, I hate you." She waved her spoon. "Whenever I need you, you are mute. Dead like a doornail. And whenever you should hold your peace, you keep ringing your head off."

She put a spoonful of vanilla yogurt into her mouth and swallowed. The stupid telephone didn't even rise to a bait like that.

"You are an instrument of torture." She put her head to one side. "I just thought I'll let you know, so you know where we stand."

The fridge started to hum; it's deep bass sound reverberated in the silent kitchen.

Cathy finished her yogurt. She made a dabbing motion with her spoon toward the unresponsive rectangle in front of her.

"Tell me, why doesn't he call me?"

Her voice sounded loud in the empty room.

She licked off her spoon. "If he called me, I wouldn't have to make a decision. It wouldn't be my fault if I couldn't resist him, would it?"

The fridge fell silent again. All she could hear was the faint humming of the traffic on the distant I-90.

Cathy stirred and threw the phone a look. Her throat

hurt and for some reason, her eyes burned too. "You're not very responsive tonight, are you?"

No reply.

The silence crept closer, engulfed her, swallowed her. All at once, something inside her broke. Cathy dropped her spoon, burrowed her head in her arms and cried.

At the beginning, she'd thought she would get over it. They'd only spent a few hours together, nothing much, really. But she couldn't forget the way he'd looked at her. She'd felt so at home. With him, she was able to be herself.

She didn't send any other job applications. There was nothing advertised that seemed to fit her even remotely.

Life dawdled on, each day longer than the day before. Only one thing worth mentioning happened. On Thursday, when Dan had gone out to his training, Cathy made herself scrambled eggs. They weren't quite as good as Dan's, but at least they were edible.

A week later, the heat wave that had gripped the Pacific Northwest abated. It ended with torrents of rain and washed away the dust from the streets like an impatient arm clearing a table in one wide sweep.

At six o'clock, it was almost dark. Cathy parked her car at the east of Coeur d'Alene Park, then jumped out and ran for the door of her house, covering her head with her coat. The smell of wet asphalt engulfed her. Her feet splashed through puddles, but louder than that, she could hear the gurgling sound of the water finding its way into the open cracks of the sun-baked earth next to the street.

With a whirl, she ran through the door and slammed it shut. Whew.

Then she froze. A letter sat on the sideboard, with her name printed on it. An official letter from the Convention Center. Her hand dripping with water, she ripped it open.

"Dear Ms Albray," it read, "we regret to inform you we have found another candidate for . . ."

Cathy stopped reading. A drop of rain ran down her nose and dropped from the tip straight to the floor. Another one sneaked beneath her hair and crept down her back with clammy hands. She shivered.

All hope gone.

This was the lid on the coffin called Seattle.

She should have known. She'd not expected anything else, had she? Not after the disaster at Frances' party.

The letter felt soggy in her hand. She crumbled it into a ball and dropped it into the wastepaper basket.

She had to find a hole to crawl into.

Now.

"I think I'll go to bed early tonight." She went to her room, threw off her clothes, and burrowed deep into her bed.

Chapter Ten

T he next week was the worst Cathy had ever lived through. She tried to think of new ways to get to Seattle, but all she could see was her own inadequacy. Then, one rainy evening, the telephone rang.

"Hi, this is Cathy."

"Cathy. David Bernett here."

Cathy drew a sharp breath. Mick's stepfather. Had anything happened to Mick? Was he in the hospital, maybe, asking for her? Was he . . .

"I'm glad I've reached you. How are you?"

Cathy's knees threatened to buckle under. "I'm fine." Her voice sounded as if she was having a heart attack. He wouldn't waste time on being polite if it was an emergency, would he? Belatedly, she remembered her manners. "And you?" *And Mick?*

"Just fine." He didn't sound as if he was the bearer of

bad news. Maybe Mick wasn't about to die after all. "I've got a job proposal to make to you," Dave said.

Cathy sat down on the floor with a thud.

"Are you still there?"

"Yes." Her voice sounded strangled. "Yes. Go on."

"I'm not sure if Mick told you I'm the managing director of a company called Be-Light. We're doing custom-made lamps for all kinds of purposes. Mainly office stuff, but a large and growing part of the company is doing public lighting for outdoors and indoors. Parks, restaurants, and so on."

Cathy made some sound in her throat, to tell him she was still listening. Her fingers were clamped on the phone so tight, it hurt.

"The biggest chunk of growth we have is derived from exports, particularly to the UK. We have our own subsidiary there. They are our European headquarters, and I'm looking for someone to manage our international exports. I wondered if you would like to take that job."

Cathy's mouth dropped open. She closed it with an effort. "Oh." It sounded like a croak.

"I thought of you because you mentioned you were applying for a job in Seattle. But of course, you may already have an offer from the Convention Center?"

"No." In her haste to correct him, it came out flat and dry. "Oh, no."

"Do you think you might be interested?"

"Yes!" If eloquence was needed for the job, Dave

would have second thoughts in a minute. She cleared her throat. "It sounds very interesting."

"Great," Dave said. "I'd like you to come over so we can discuss what I have in mind. What do you think?"

Cathy pulled up her knees to her chest and hugged them hard with her free arm. "That sounds good to me."

"All right. Do you think you can make it for next Friday?"

"Sure." If he'd asked her to board a space shuttle in five minutes, she'd have done it willingly, barefoot and all.

"Very good. I'm looking forward to seeing you again. I'll put you through to my secretary now; she can arrange the details of your flight, is that okay?"

Cathy opened her mouth and closed it again. "Sure."

Dave hung up and Cathy heard a female voice. She collected her wits sufficiently to arrange the flight and even remembered to note Dave's telephone number, then she switched off the telephone and placed it on the floor next to her as if it held the crown jewels.

Wow.

This was it.

Her one big chance.

She leaned back and grinned like an idiot at the bare wall in front of her. All of a sudden, a thought shot through her and made her sit bolt upright. What if Mick had asked Dave to do it? What if this wasn't a real of-fer, but just a . . . a gift of compassion?

How humiliating.

But surely Mick would not go to these lengths, if he didn't even call once? Cathy rubbed her shoulder. Two more days. How was she going to make it until Friday?

"Ladies and Gentlemen, we are approaching Seattle. Please fasten your seat belts, fold up the table in front of you, and put the back of your seat in an upright position."

Cathy's hands shook as she checked the seat belt. Swallowing hard, she stared out of the window. The plane slid down and broke through the clouds. Mount Rainier greeted her like a friend. Cathy held her breath.

The plane eased deeper. Below, Cathy caught a glimpse of Puget Sound flying past before the pilot turned the plane in a wide circle and tilted it at an angle that hid the ground from view. Now, only clouds filled the sky. Different shades of gray pasted one over another; they looked like a rough sheet above her.

She was almost there.

She had to be cool.

She had to be in control.

Maybe Mick knew she was coming. Maybe he would pick her up at the airport. Her heart beat faster. No, probably not. Dave had told her to get a taxi.

This would not do. She gripped her armrests with both hands and tried to calm herself.

"Are you all right?"

A flight attendant bent over her. Her black hair was bound back in a ponytail, emphasizing her curved eyebrows.

Cathy forced a smile. "Yeah. Thanks." She liked flying. The idea of leaving everything behind, of breaking all bonds and just going somewhere and starting a new life had always fascinated her.

Now she had the chance.

If only it worked out.

If only she was good enough.

The plane touched the ground. Immediately, it started to roar like an irritated tiger and shot to the end of the tarmac where the pilot forced it with an iron hand to calm down and meekly roll toward the gate.

Sea-Tac Airport. The name was magic to Cathy. Feeling as if she were dreaming, she plucked her bag from beneath her seat and strode to the exit.

Though she told herself she was a fool, she couldn't stop scanning the waiting crowd when she came out of the security zone.

Her heart missed a beat.

Dark-blond hair, flopping forward.

But when he turned his head, her heart sank. He didn't look in the least like Mick. Her disappointment was so out of proportion, she had to shake herself. With her lips pressed together, she hurried to find a taxi.

When the taxi driver finally pulled up in front of a low building, she took a deep breath. Ten minutes to go. Perfect. She looked up the dark orange brick front. It had been built in a time when even an office building did not go unadorned. At the very top, Cathy could make out a decorative border that covered the whole length. Three stories high and broad, it was more squat than elegant, but when she entered the building, she held her breath. She stood in a showroom, lit by hundreds of visible and invisible lights. The high ceiling, painted white, contrasted with the dark red brick of the natural walls.

"Can I help you?"

Cathy jumped and swung round to the slim woman in front of her. "I'm Catherine Albray."

The woman smiled. Her suit was molded to her figure, not a crease out of place. "Welcome to Be-Light," she said. "David is already waiting for you."

Cathy was led into a meeting room on the third floor. "David will be here in a minute." The slim woman disappeared with another smile. Left alone, Cathy's eyes were drawn to the large windows. She was surprised to see water. The sun broke through the clouds and reflected off the surface, throwing a dancing shadow onto the ceiling, before hiding behind the clouds again.

"That's Elliott Bay," she heard David say behind her.

Cathy whirled around. "Hello, David." He was impressive in his dark suit and white shirt. Cathy was glad she'd put on her best business outfit.

He smiled at her. "Welcome to Be-Light. It's nice to see you." She had forgotten his uneven eyebrows and their sarcastic tilt.

"Thank you for the invitation." She felt breathless and shy.

"Did you have a good trip?"

"Perfect, thank you." Her mouth was dry.

David looked at her as if he wanted to say something, then smiled and made an inviting motion with his hand. "Why don't you sit down? Would you like some coffee?"

"That would be lovely."

David filled a fragile bone china cup, and as he passed it to Cathy, he said, "Should I explain what I have in mind?"

Cathy nodded. "Yes, please."

David leaned back and crossed his legs. "Be-Light was founded some forty years ago. It started with standard lighting for parks and official sites. By now, it has developed into a brand name that stands for modern, elegant lighting solutions, indoors and outdoors. I've been with the company for ten years now. In the last few years, we have expanded internationally." He leaned back, at his ease, and put an arm on the back of the chair next to him. "It's a real challenge, what with different regulations, not to mention plugs and voltages, but we find it's worth it. As I believe I mentioned on the phone, the most important subsidiary is based in London. The others— partly subsidiaries, partly joint ventures—are based in Berlin, Paris, Brussels, and Rome. All in all, about three thousand people work for Be-Light."

He leaned forward and folded his hands on the table. "But up to now, we don't have someone responsible for keeping in touch with our subsidiaries. Somebody who makes sure they get all the necessary information concerning new products in time. Somebody who is the first contact person, who finds out where problems are and to represent their interests over here on a permanent basis. It's a sort of export manager, if you want to."

He made a pause and searched her face.

Cathy took a deep breath. "It sounds thrilling."

David smiled. "I'm glad you say so. It's a challenging position." He hesitated, then added. "To be open with you, I have to admit there are some problems right now. The head of the European headquarters, Peter Downstable, has somehow gotten the impression we don't support him sufficiently. He is irritated about it . . . ." Dave put a hand across his mouth and stared out the window.

Cathy's stomach coiled up. Here came the hitch.

"And there is quite a lot of tension between the staff on this side and the other." He met her eyes. "A sort of English-American aversion. I need someone to change that because I don't want to lose Peter. He's a brilliant manager."

Cathy knew she had to pretend to be strong. To be a winner. But she couldn't. She had to admit it before he employed her and then found out what a mistake he'd made . . . particularly if Mick had put him up to it.

She bit her lip, then cleared her throat. "I . . . I'm sorry, Dave, but I am not exactly good at dealing with irritated people." She was shooting her one and only chance to pieces. But she couldn't leave Mick's stepfather under a wrong impression. She had lied to him before she knew him, but this was different. And if Mick had asked him to do it, it was even worse.

David looked at her, his left eyebrow even higher than usual. "Aren't you?"

Cathy answered without taking a breath, before she could lose her courage. "I know I shouldn't say so, but I am not the tough business type you'll need for that job." Rapidly, she added. "Though I would love it. It sounds fascinating."

"Good," David said, as if she hadn't spoken. "Then you have it."

Cathy bent forward. "But . . ."

He nodded. "I heard you. It's exactly what I want. I've got plenty of young bulls around who are willing to be tough. They would antagonize Peter from the first word." He leaned back and smiled at her.

Cathy was sure he had gotten it wrong. "Do you really think . . . ?"

"Positive." David's teeth gleamed in his brown face.

Cathy was perplexed. "Why? And how . . . ?"

David's gray eyes were amused. "I'll tell you why." He lifted his hand and checked off the reasons on his immaculately groomed fingers. "First, you are diplomatic and able to see two sides at the same time, even if personally involved. I saw you deal with Frances when she had that fight with Mick, and I had to hand it to you. That was well done."

Cathy didn't believe her ears. She'd never seen herself like that.

Dave continued, "Second, you have tact. You stopped the fight between me and Paul as if you had been doing it for ages." He paused and sighed. "I wish you had." He shook his head as if to clear it and turned back to his fingers.

"Third, you have charm. Any man would accept a *no* from you better than from another man or even a tactless woman."

Cathy felt her face going red.

"Fourth, you notice details about people, and you use that knowledge in a positive way."

Cathy blinked. "I don't understand."

"You asked me if I wanted a whiskey at the party because you'd seen me drinking one earlier in the evening."

Cathy knew she stared, but she couldn't help it. He remembered her every move!

He smiled at her and continued. "And fifth, you are perfect because you come across as very British, even though you are American. That will help you a lot, particularly in the beginning."

Cathy blinked. All of a sudden, she felt curiously light. If she got up now, she'd float out the window.

David grinned. "I might add you're honest and have the right educational background with your degree in business, but you know that as well as I do."

"I . . ." Her voice threatened to fail her. "Thank you."

David's glance was shrewd when he assessed her once again. Then he added. "Oh, I know you can be bullied because you hate conflict. But you can learn techniques to overcome that. It's a lot easier to learn than to acquire the skills you already have."

Cathy nodded as if it wasn't new to her. She'd just grown an inch. Was she really . . . diplomatic? Tactful? Charming? It sounded wonderful.

The rest of the day passed in a haze. David showed

her the whole building and presented her to everyone. She couldn't remember a single name afterward, with the exception of Harry Mandini. Harry was going to share an office with her. He wore a large pair of glasses that must have been the last cry in the seventies. They covered half his face and changed to a bluish tint in sunlight. Combined with a shock of black curls standing all around his head, a mouth that bisected his face by stretching from one ear to the other, and a beak of a nose, he was a sight hard to forget. "Harry is responsible for the development of new products and just a little bit crazy about any new technology." David presented him with a twinkle in his eye.

"Nice to meet you." Harry's voice was too soft and low for his bulk. "David is always so down-to-earth." He pulled a face. "He didn't even allow a little light show linked to my computer that would change the color of the overhead light every time I hit my mouse."

Cathy shuddered. "Sounds funky."

David laughed.

A sheep started to *baa* somewhere. Cathy whipped around and stared behind her. "That's my mobile phone." Harry grinned and ambled away.

"Will you stay with Mick for the weekend or are you planning to return right home?" David asked when he said good-bye.

So Mick hadn't told them about anything! Did he know about the job offer at all? Cathy rubbed her left shoulder. "I . . . um . . . I'm going home tonight."

David hesitated, but then his face cleared and he

said, "Right, I forgot he has that big job from Nicole, so I guess he won't have any time anyway. It's a pity, but now that you know it's only going to be three weeks before you move over, he's probably—"

Cathy froze. "Nicole?"

David shot her a look. "Yeah. Her partner has that huge property on Bainbridge Island. Surely Mick told you?"

Cathy dropped her eyes. "Oh, that one."

Dave led her to the door. "It seems they are planning to redo the whole garden, and for some reason, it's got to be real quick, so he works there day and night."

The floor was tilting beneath her feet.

"At least that's what he told his mother." David's smile was a little dry. "I won't ask you if it's true. But maybe you can persuade him to call her next week. She's not heard from him since her birthday."

"Hm." Cathy stared at the floor.

He held out his hand. "Thank you, Cathy. I'm glad you accepted my offer and I am looking forward to welcoming you to my staff."

Cathy gripped his hand. "Thanks. Me too. I mean, I'm very happy."

She managed it through the door without stumbling and almost fell into the taxi. She'd done it.

She had a job!

A wonderful job.

A well-paid job.

So why was she feeling exhausted, even blue? Why didn't she jump sky-high?

She tried to push the image of Mick working night and day in Nicole's garden far away. Could it be the whole setup of her being his girl had served to make Nicole jealous?

No, that was unthinkable.

Cathy shook herself.

They were almost at the airport. She had to go home again. But this time, it was different. She returned with a prize. And the knowledge that she would soon come back. It was a better feeling altogether. If only . . . She sighed. Why, oh why didn't he call?

"So you're moving in with that lover of yours?" Dan buttered his toast. He had not been in when she arrived late in the evening from Seattle, so she had to wait until breakfast to break the news.

"No! How on earth did you get that impression?" Cathy stirred her coffee until it slopped over.

"Well, he's the new protector, isn't he?"

Cathy dropped her spoon. "I do not need a protector." She spoke through clenched teeth. "All I need is to stand on my own. I got a job. And I will find a room for myself. It has nothing to do with Mick."

Dan yawned. "Well, good luck with it. Tell me when you move in with him."

Cathy jumped up and knocked against the table so hard, her coffee sloshed over. "You're detestable!" She ran to her room. Slamming the door shut, she threw herself down on her bed. Tears started to spill down her cheeks. How could he? It was such an achievement to have found a new job. She balled her hands into fists. She would show him.

Chapter Eleven

"It's a reeel beautiful room," Mr. Garelli said and pushed the dark brown door wide open.

Cathy had already spent two weeks in Seattle, in a bed-and-breakfast close to work. This was the third Saturday in a row she spent house-hunting, and she was sick of it.

Mr. Garelli stepped to the side to allow her to go inside, but just when she inched past him, he got closer again. Cathy backed up to the door frame to put some distance between them. The room smelled musty and of garlic, though the latter probably came from the owner, who still stood much too close for comfort.

It was a single room, with a tiny window going out to a backyard. A Formica table stood in a corner, a rickety chair in front. The bed had probably known the contemporaries of Chief Seattle. Maybe the mattress too, judging by the way it sagged between the posts. Cathy felt her skin crawling. She looked up. An orange lampshade managed to hang by sheer force of will around a bulb in the ceiling, its tassels full of dust and cobwebs. In the upper left-hand corner, a dark patch showed on the wallpaper that had begun to peel off the wall.

Cathy forced a smile on her face. "Thank you very much." She tried to sound resolute and moved to the door. "I'll think about it."

He barred her way. All of a sudden, Cathy knew she should never have come up with him. His sleeveless shirt had dark patches on the front, and his sagging trousers were only held up by an old belt that was going to fall into pieces any minute. "What? What? You not see bathroom. It is good, very good." Mr. Garelli formed a *O* with his thumb and fingers and kissed the tips.

Cathy drew herself up. She was almost as tall as he was. "No. Thank you. I have to be on my way."

The owner bent forward and hissed, "No good enough? You too elegant for my beeeautiful room? What is wrong, eh? You tell me what is wrong! It is good, reeel good!"

The smell of garlic out of his mouth, mixed with something Cathy did not want to think about, was so overpowering, she jerked back. He followed her and shook a finger an inch from her nose. Horrified, Cathy watched him talking himself into a frenzy. "You say it is bad? You tell me, a Garelli, my beeeautiful room is bad?

You go see somewhere else! You go find out! There is not better. No better, I say you!"

All of a sudden, something snapped inside her. How dare he? She balled her hands into fists. "Yes, I do say it is bad. It's dirty, it's moldy, and it's furnished with the worst furniture I've ever seen. If I dared to offer a room like that to my worst enemy, I would hide under a bed for shame!" She threw a glance at the sad object in question and turned back to him in a fury. "But not under this bed, Mr. Garelli, as I would be likely to contract several diseases at once!"

She pushed the speechless man out of the way and clattered down the steps. Back at her car, she found her knees were shaking.

What a horrible guy.

If only she could ask somebody to help her. She bit her lips. If Mick were here, he would comfort her now. She wouldn't have to face everything on her own.

That's what you wanted, a voice inside her said.

Yeah, but I didn't want it to be like this.

You want to be independent, you take it all. The voice was unperturbed.

Oh, shut up!

Cathy started the motor so hard, she almost broke off the key. She wished she could wash her hands somewhere. Had she touched anything at that lousy place? Her scalp itched. So much for the Blue Sky Apartments in Ballard. It meant another week at the bed-and-breakfast. She had to find something soon, or her budget was going to run out. A tear rolled down her face. With clenched teeth, she wiped it away. She would make it. There had to be some nice place out there where she could stay.

"I can't believe there's such a nasty Italian in Seattle." Harry crossed his hands behind his head. He leaned back in his chair and put both feet on his desk. The rain was weeping against the window, hiding the view of Elliott Bay and its concrete borderline behind a gray curtain, but Cathy's table was covered in a soft pool of light by her desk lamp.

He smiled at Cathy. "As I said, you're always welcome to stay with me, you know. I have a broad bed, a gentle cat, a good toaster. . . ."

Cathy grinned. They'd been through this several times already, and the longer she refused, the more seductive the details he put into his proposals. "Your soles need to be redone."

Harry lifted one foot and turned it to look underneath. His huge glasses blinked in the light. "You're exaggerating, as usual." He sighed with his soft voice said, "A little hole is not . . . ouch!" He stiffened, then stopped moving altogether and almost doubled over.

Cathy lifted her eyebrows, but she knew him well enough by now. "Did you learn that at your yoga class last night? Doesn't look too healthy to me."

"Stop laughing and help me up." His voice sounded strangled. "I believe something got stuck in my spine. A vital nerve."

Cathy ambled over and gripped his arm.

"No!" Harry's voice rose in a wail. "Not like that! Be careful! How can you look so nice and be so brutal?"

"Appearances can be misleading."

"What's going on?" David's voice came from the door.

Harry straightened with surprising speed, but kept his hand in the small of his back.

"Are you hurt, Harry?"

"He was just showing me the most relaxing part of his yoga class last night and something got stuck in his spine." Cathy kept her face straight. "But your entry miraculously healed him right away."

Harry grunted. "When I said I wanted a nice colleague to share my room, I didn't count on getting someone like her, David."

David smiled. "You said you wanted a beautiful woman, intelligent, interesting, . . . I forget what else, the list was quite long."

Harry sighed and waved a languid hand. "Yeah, she may have all that. But you never mentioned she has no heart."

David lifted his eyebrows. "I can't recall that on the list."

Cathy chuckled.

Harry crossed his arms on the desk in front of him and dropped his head onto them. "Two against one. I stand no chance." His voice was muffled.

"Life is hard and cruel, dear." Cathy returned to her desk.

Harry lifted his head. "Did you hear that? Who could stand a woman like that?"

David came up to Harry's desk and put a folder on it. "Well, since I hope she'll be my daughter-in-law soon, there must have been one at least."

Cathy froze. She felt the blood draining from her face.

Harry opened his eyes wide and stared at her. "Really? Your son must have an indestructible ego, David."

David's smile deepened, but he did not reply. Instead, he said, "I came to ask about the development of the Burlington-Brown lamp. He has asked me to call him back, and I first wanted to know where we stand."

Harry's eyes started to shine. He took out a huge plotted sheet with a technical drawing and spread it on his desk. "It's almost finished, and I love it. Rob and I just don't agree if we should put a dome head nut here, or rather . . ."

Cathy stopped listening and turned back to the sheets on her desk. She had asked for a list of figures, showing her which products sold best in which countries. By calling her partners in the subsidiaries, she had learned a lot about the different lighting systems and regional differences as well. It fascinated her, but right now, she found it hard to concentrate.

She had barely seen Dave in the last weeks and somehow, she had kidded herself that it didn't matter if she was Mick's girl or not. How on earth was she going to explain to Dave there was not going to be any marriage at all? Would he resent it, having offered her the job under the impression she would be part of the family? What if she hurt his family pride? Cathy rubbed her left shoulder. Would he sack her?

When David had left, Harry folded the drawing with care, then sat back and stared at her. "Well. Here I am, eating my heart out, telling you night and day that my one and only longing is for you, and you never even mention you're engaged!"

Cathy put her finger on the column she had just tried to add for the fifth time and lifted her head. "Harry, you tell every single woman you meet she's the most fascinating person on earth."

"And so she is!" He laughed.

"Until you see the next one coming around the corner." Cathy picked up her mug and finished her coffee.

"I'm not as crude as that!" He looked hurt.

"No, you're always so charming, one might even believe you . . ." She nodded.

"Thank you."

". . . if one tends to have delusions."

He shook his head. "You are much too down-to-earth. It must be that English heritage in you."

Cathy was glad he'd stopped talking about her so-called engagement. "Well, if I were half Italian like you, I might sing a serenade to the beauty of your black curls."

"I'd like that."

"I'm sure you would."

"Do you sing for your fiancé?"

Cathy's smile froze.

"Uh-oh." Harry lifted both hands to the ceiling and dropped them again. "Forbidden ground, eh?" He wagged his head. "So there is a heart after all." He sighed. "But not for me. Poor lonely me."

"You're an idiot." Cathy smiled and returned to the sheet in front of her.

Harry wasn't so easily distracted. "So you're going to be one of the family, eh?"

Cathy made a noncommitting sound in her throat.

"Dave likes that."

Her head came up. "What do you mean?"

Harry waved a hand in the air. "Dave is a firm believer in connections and personal contact. He always prefers to work with friends and family, rather than with business partners only."

Cathy swallowed. "Right. But it's not always necessary, is it? You for example aren't connected, are you?"

Harry grinned. "My father went to school with him."

Cathy groaned.

Harry shook his head, misunderstanding her. "I know. Imagine, they discuss me on the golf course. But luckily, my old man hasn't had any complaints. So far."

He got up and ambled to the door. "I'll go get some coffee. You want some too?"

Cathy shook her head. How on earth was she going to manage? She tried to continue working, but her fears loomed above her. She kept hearing her own voice. "I don't want to end up homeless in Seattle." And then Dan's voice. "You'll never make it."

All at once, Harry stormed back into the office. "Cathy, I need your help." For once, there was no smile on his face.

"What is it?"

"That absolute so-and-so Burlington-Brown insists on

a meeting tomorrow morning, to discuss the last details of that whole light show he's thinking up, and I can't go."

Cathy frowned. "Didn't you take tomorrow off?"

He nodded so hard, his curls bounced. "Yeah, it's my parent's thirtieth wedding anniversary." He made a wide circle with both arms. "The whole family is present, all my brothers and sisters, cousins, aunts, uncles . . ."

"I get it." Cathy chuckled. "All Seattle will be blocked with Mandinis."

"Yeah. My mother hasn't stopped talking about it since Christmas. There's absolutely no way I can stay away. But I'm lucky . . ." He bent forward and smiled his most charming smile. "I have a colleague I can send instead."

"What?" Cathy shot up. "I don't know a single thing about those lamps!"

He hurried around the desk and put his arm around her shoulders. "I'll teach you all you need to know."

Cathy shuddered. "I'm lost when it comes to electricity. I know it can spark, that's all."

"That's a start." He glanced at her sideways. "If you know that much, is there any way you will find a spark between us?"

Cathy rolled her eyes and took his arm off her shoulders. "Behave yourself."

Harry moaned. "All the time you blight my happiness. I could end up in the gutter, for all you care."

"You want to end up at that party, so you'd better start telling me more about your lamp. Did you tell David you want me to go instead?"

Harry sat down on her desk and swung his legs. "He thinks it's a good idea."

"No kidding."

"Yes! After all, it's more a courtesy visit than anything else."

Cathy shook her head. "You don't usually go to see customers. That's not part of your job, is it?"

Harry sighed. "Gosh, no. But Burlington-Brown is the biggest bigshot in Seattle real estate business. He's a VIP. As vippy as one can get. Right now—I should say since last year—he is redesigning his private park, light and all. We made a special model for him and developed special lighting effects and whatnots."

"Sounds complicated."

"He drove us wild. But now it's basically finished."

"So what does he want from you now?"

"I believe he wants more lamps than originally planned due to some changes in design, and now he'd like to discuss the possible positions." He shrugged. "It's easy. Just make sure you don't interrupt him, and agree to everything he says. He'll love that."

"Sounds like a piece of cake." Cathy took a deep breath. "I'm good at saying yes."

Harry's broad mouth stretched into a wolfish smile. "So you'll move in with me?"

Cathy got up. "You'd be scared to the tips of your toes if I ever consented," she said. "Now stop dawdling and show me those drawings of the Burlington-Brown lamp."

She took the drawing home that night and tried to

memorize every detail, though Harry had noted all the technical data on a sheet, so she could look them up tomorrow during the meeting.

Her tiny room still smelled of the Chinese takeaway she had grabbed on her way home. Cathy got up and opened the window wide. It had stopped raining. The air was soft and sweet, if she did not count the exhaust fumes coming up from Yesler Way. All of a sudden, she knew she had to get out.

Now.

Cathy put on her shorts and a wide T-shirt, then her running shoes. Her fingers ran down the smooth material at the side. How she loved them. Her mood lifted already. It would do her good to get out and run it out of her system. Her loneliness was hard to bear tonight, not to mention her fear of tomorrow or her worry about finding a room. Running would make it better.

She sped out of the house and turned right, to go up the hill. Kobe Terrace Park was just a few blocks away. On her first evening, she'd checked the map for a place to go running and had been delighted to discover one so close to her bed-and-breakfast.

When she passed through the gate, she took a deep breath and started running. There. She felt better already. She loved the peace of this little island in the middle of a roaring town. It seemed to be a different world, particularly with all the Asians around. Cathy imagined she had gone on a trip to Asia, all on her own. It sent a little tickle of adventure down her spine. One day, she would . . .

Suddenly, a little Japanese girl rushed up from the left and crossed her way without looking left nor right. Cathy swerved to the side to avoid hitting her. The girl ran on, never even noticing the accident she had almost caused. Cathy followed her with her eyes. Her black pigtail was adorned with a huge red bow, bouncing with every step. Behind her, Cathy saw the girl's mother throw up her hands, then make a gesture that seemed to say sorry.

Cathy smiled at her and ran on. She heard Mick's voice again, in his van. "I'd want a kid, preferably with a nose like yours." What on earth had made him say that, if he neither called nor made the slightest effort to get in touch with her again.

Her feet pounded the ground. From somewhere, she got a whiff of dried grass. The smell of summer. It was soon going to be over. She could see autumn approaching in the color of the leaves on the trees. Maybe she should call Mick. After all, she'd proven she could stand on her own now, hadn't she?

Oh no, the nasty voice inside her replied, *you don't even have a room yet.*

But I have a job, and I've been very independent for almost three weeks, her other self replied.

True emancipation, the voice mocked. *What a record to show!*

Well, it's more than I ever managed before. She panted a little.

Don't be so stupid to give it up again before you really start.

Cathy scowled at the blameless snow-viewing lantern to her left. On her first evening in the park, she had stopped and read the inscription on it, to know what the funny structure meant. She ran on at an accelerated pace.

How long would she have to live on her own until she would feel she had made it? Wasn't it stupid to clutch at this fixed idea of hers, when she had met someone who might well be the perfect partner? Wasn't she destroying a chance of happiness and following a mere fantasy?

She shook her head to clear it and ran on. Her breath was coming in gasps now. Oh, how she wanted to call him. How she wanted to hear his whiskey voice. She'd last seen him eight weeks and two days ago, and still, she couldn't stop thinking about him. Wasn't that a sign too?

She finished her two rounds and came to a stop. Her chest seemed to explode with every ragged breath she took. She bent down and placed her hands on her thighs to ease the breathing. After a few minutes, she stretched, shook out her legs and dragged herself home. Running hadn't helped much today. She still felt unsettled, and that blasted Burlington-Brown meeting tomorrow morning didn't make things better.

In the hope to get a good night's sleep before the meeting, she went to bed early, but kept tossing and turning. She'd expected to run across Mick somewhere in Seattle, and the idea had filled her with excitement and dread.

Now, after three weeks, it dawned on her that Seattle

was not a village where one would meet everybody eventually. They might never again meet by chance. Fate had helped once. It wasn't going to happen again. If she wanted to see him, she would have to make a decision. But what was right?

Exasperated, she punched her cushion. She remembered the fresh smell of Mick's cushion. He used a different laundry detergent than she did. She would never know what it was.

She shook her head with a half sob, half laugh. Really. What next? Did it matter what laundry detergent he used? She had to get a grip on herself. If even his laundry detergent mattered, she was in no state to keep her independence, was she?

That's what she wanted.

That's what she needed.

Nothing else.

The next morning, she arrived with time to spare at the Burlington-Brown property. Situated in the Denny Blaine neighborhood at the shore of Lake Washington, she knew enough of Seattle by now to expect something luxurious. But the wrought-iron gate still intimidated her, and it took a few minutes before she could bring herself to press down the button situated inside the mouth of a bronze lion. Walking up the gravel drive, she told herself she should not have parked her car outside, but she hadn't expected a trip that dragged on for about a mile before she even caught a glimpse of the house. When she did, she stopped dead.

It wasn't a house, it was a sort of mini-castle. The

worst she had ever seen, though. Maybe Burlington-Brown had visited the castle of Versailles a long time ago, then Venice, then Buckingham palace. Then he must have had a stomach problem or something, and the result of his mixed impressions had been the foundation for his house. She did not doubt it was his own design. No architect could do something like it if he ever hoped to get another job. Frances' house had intimidated her with sheer wealth and good taste—Burlington-Brown's house made her want to laugh or to invite a kindergarten class in. Kids would love it. They would play Beauty and the Beast, Dragon and Dwarfs, a thousand delighted games. She was still struggling to subdue her grin into a formal smile when the arched door opened with a swishing sound. A man whose form reminded her of a large ball peered at her. The light reflected off the pink dome that was his head. Cathy's eyes were drawn to his legs. He wore knickerbockers, checkered in green and orange. His socks were a matching orange, so was his T-shirt. Cathy blinked, then revised her first judgment. Not Buckingham Palace. Edinburgh Castle. Unless he was the butler. She looked up again and met his amused eyes.

"Quite an outfit, eh?" The ball paraded in front of her like a peacock.

Cathy smiled. Definitely not the butler. Burlington-Brown himself.

"It sure is." She stretched out her hand. "I'm Catherine Albray from Be-Light."

The ball gripped her hand and pumped it up and down.

"Yes, David already told me about you." He pulled at her hand, to make her come in. "Come in, come in, we want to start immediately."

The ball led her through an arched hall that gave her the impression she was in church. It even smelled of incense. Cathy tiptoed after him and tried not to breathe. Burlington-Brown threw open a heavy door and motioned her into a study with carved oak wainscoting all the way up to the ceiling. A strong smell of leather pervaded the dark room. In the middle resided a gleaming walnut table that could accommodate twenty people. Its massive legs ended in claws feet taken off a model dinosaur.

A tall man stood next to one chair and frowned at a spreadsheet that covered the whole end of the table. He lifted his head when they came in. For an instant, he was outlined like a cloud with a silver lining against the sunlight that tried to enter the gloomy room though the windows behind him.

Cathy's heart missed a beat. It couldn't be Mick.

He lifted his hand and pushed back the hair that had flopped forward into his face.

She knew that gesture. She'd dreamed of it so often.

Chapter Twelve

Her knees started to tremble.

She'd been so stupid. Mick was a landscape architect, didn't she know that? What was more natural than to work together with Be-Light, the company his stepfather managed?

She'd never expected to run into him in the course of her work.

"Mick, you've started already." Burlington-Brown towed her up to the table. "This is Catherine. I hear she's engaged to be married to one of David's sons, so you'd better stay on her good side, otherwise you might not get as many jobs as you used to with Be-Light."

Cathy felt the color draining from her face. She must be asleep, having a nightmare. Surely?

Mick jerked once, then turned to stone. When he stretched out his hand in slow motion, it looked as if he was carved of wood and didn't yet know how to move properly. Like a stranger, he said, his voice unrecognizable, "Nice to meet you."

Cathy gave him her hand, unable to utter a word. He barely touched her, then dropped her hand again as if it were unsanitary.

Cathy's throat started to ache.

"You've only been with Be-Light a short time, haven't you?" Burlington-Brown asked.

"Three weeks." Cathy had to squeeze out the words.

Mick's eyes widened. So he'd had no idea she had moved to Seattle. She'd wake up soon. Her alarm clock would ring in a minute.

Burlington-Brown was already bending over the map. "Look here, Vandenholt, I believe we have to change the alley. The way it is right now, it doesn't allow a full view of the house. If we changed it and it ran from over here"—his chubby finger jabbed at a point on the map—"to over there"—he drew a straight line across the paper—"it would be better."

Mick frowned and bent forward. "I'll show Catherine the general layout first, okay?"

Burlington-Brown lifted his head, surprised. "I'm sorry, Catherine, I get so excited I keep forgetting my manners."

Together, they bent over the map. Mick's sleeve brushed Cathy's arm. She swallowed.

"That's the mansion." Burlington-Brown indicated a form on the paper. "Over here is the alley that crosses the whole property." Burlington-Brown pointed at something that looked like a twisted rope with dotted points to the left and right. "As you can see, the alley is the most important thing about the design. It leads across the whole property, but it does not offer a view of the house anywhere."

A good thing too, Cathy suppressed a grin. Mick had probably known exactly what he was doing when he planned it. Loudly, she said, "Yes, I see what you mean."

Burlington-Brown nodded so hard, his head reminded Cathy more than ever of a bouncing ball. "Now if we changed the direction of the alley at this point right here and if we put the trees a little bit farther apart, it would be just right."

Cathy tried to concentrate. Harry had explained to her they had developed a lamp like a long flute, widening at the bottom and at the top. The lamps would be fixed onto each tree of the alley, to shoot a bright torch of light both up and down at the same time. She felt Mick moving next to her. It made her skin tingle. All of a sudden, she found it difficult to breathe.

Burlington-Brown fixed her with a stare. "How far does the light reach? Would it be possible to move the trees farther apart?"

Cathy's mind went blank. Harry had said something about the distance. What was it? Trying to gain time, she said, "Well, you know they were designed to reach farther than ordinary lights." That much she could remember. "But I am not sure . . ."

Burlington-Brown frowned. "Surely you can tell me the maximum distance?"

"The maximum distance is a mute point in this case," Mick said, "as the direction of the light is not horizontal, but vertical."

Cathy sighed with relief.

Burlington-Brown shook his head. "But it does pool at the bottom. All I want to know is how much."

Cathy nodded and clicked open her briefcase with trembling fingers. "Sure. That's an important point. Let me just check it." She opened her file and took out the sheet with the technical data. There it was. Phew. "It's approximately five feet across."

"But that's not enough!" Burlington-Brown almost jumped on the spot.

"You don't want the whole place floodlighted, do you?" Mick saved her again. "The whole point is in creating little surprises all along the way by offering a constant change from light to dark."

The ball gave an infinitesimal nod, then rolled up the map and strutted to the door. "We have to see it on-site." He motioned them to follow.

Cathy crammed her papers back into her briefcase and hurried to the door Mick held open. "Thank you."

He nodded, his face blank. Cathy tried to take a deep breath, but it hurt.

With their backs to the house, the place looked a lot better. The ball rolled in front and lead them across the property. Bulldozers were already busy leveling the ground. Their droning made it difficult to talk. Dark brown earth was piled up in regular intervals. It smelled fresh and reminded her of autumn. Cathy had trouble to keep up with the men in her high-heeled shoes. When she stopped for a minute and looked up, she found herself staring into Mick's lion eyes. His gaze was fierce, hungry. Furious too. Cathy stumbled and would have fallen if he had not gripped her arm and steadied her. The warmth of his hands on her skin caused her stomach to flutter, even though he dropped her arm as soon as she had found her equilibrium.

The ball stopped and opened the map again. "There. This is the place I mean. If we gave the alley a different angle, it would offer a magnificent view."

Cathy wheeled around and shuddered. The castle stood in full splendor in front of them. She hadn't realized there were at least fifteen turrets plastered to the back.

Mick shook his head. "I believe the version we have right now shows the castle to more advantage."

Cathy hid a grin. How adroitly phrased. To show the castle from its best side, you had to hide it under a giant cloth.

Burlington-Brown didn't want to hear that. Cathy could see resistance building up in him, and all of a sudden, she knew how to handle him.

"I believe you have to present the castle as a big, breathtaking finale," she said. "It should come all of a sudden, and it should make everybody gasp with surprise."

Burlington-Brown jumped up and down, his eyes shining. "Yes, that's how it should be!"

Mick stared at her as if she had lost her mind.

Cathy smiled. "To achieve that, you have to hide it

from view until the very end. Build up the tension, so to speak."

The orange flecks in Mick's eyes started to show. He had caught on.

Cathy checked the map. When Mick had shown her the map, she'd noticed something . . . yes, there it was. "That's a hill, isn't it?" She pointed at a dotted line.

"Yes." Mick smiled. "It's going to be a little bit farther to the left." He pointed in the direction. "Over there. It will offer a view of Lake Washington on the other side."

Cathy nodded. "Great." Then she faced Burlington-Brown. "Wouldn't that be a perfect place to make a pavilion? It could be the end of the alley, leading up to it. From over there, you would have a fantastic view of the lake and, at the other side, the castle. At night, it could be illuminated."

Burlington-Brown jumped up and down. "Yes! That's a wonderful idea. We could have a moat all around it, with a bridge."

Cathy gasped. *Why not add a gigantic stone dragon, to guard the whole show*? But she was careful not to say her thought out loud. She was beginning to get the ball's measure and knew he would jump at anything as long as it was hideous. Mick would kill her if she destroyed his garden.

She stole a look at him. He was amused, she could tell by the slant of his eyebrows, though his face was serious, bent down to listen to Burlington-Browns words.

An hour later, Cathy's patience started to flag. It was hard to be tactful all the time, and she could see no end in sight. Burlington-Brown enjoyed discussing his plans over and over again, jumping from one idea to the next, then back again. Two eternal hours later, he closed the arched castle door behind them, after having dithered on the threshold for another twenty minutes. Cathy waited until they were well out of earshot, then she let out a long sigh. "Phew. What a guy. Do you have many customers like him?"

"I'm thankful to say he's the worst."

Cathy grinned at him. He returned her smile. Then, all of a sudden, his smile faded and he looked away.

Cathy bit her lips. He had blocked her out. Summoning up all her courage, she said, "I still have a little time before I have to return to the office. Why don't we go to Starbucks and grab a coffee?"

Mick shook his head. "Sorry, I don't have any time today." He turned his back to her. "I'll be seeing you." He hurried away, his long legs striding away as if she was pursuing him. Cathy stood rooted to the ground and stared after him. Something large blocked her throat. Her eyes followed him along the drive that turned left behind the castle. She'd not seen it when she had arrived. Almost hidden by some rhododendron bushes, she caught a glimpse of his van.

This is your own fault. A voice inside her whispered. *You wanted to be on your own.*

I wanted to be independent.

Yeah. Big deal. You're too full of yourself to see when a good thing is happening to you. Now you've driven him away.

No! She felt like crying.

Oh yes. What kind of man would wait so long, anyway? Besides, Nicole wasn't far away from him the last weeks. You've seen the result.

Oh shut up! She whipped around and ran to her car.

As soon as she got home that night, Cathy took out her running shoes with clenched teeth. She needed friends to go out with. Tons of them. Without partners, so she wouldn't have to watch them together. She'd best join a club.

She put on her shorts and T-shirt and ran downstairs, waving in passing at her landlady who just came up. "Good evening, Mrs. Brown. I'm going for a run." She hoped against hope for a friendly answer.

"Wait!" Her landlady held onto the railing to sustain her wobbling masses and gasped for breath.

Cathy stopped in her tracks. "Yes?"

"A regular customer is gonna come next Wednesday. You need to move out on Tuesday."

Cathy stared at her. "But I . . ."

"You never said you would stay so long." Mrs. Brown clutched the railing as if she could not stand without it. It creaked a protest.

Something must have shown in Cathy's face because she added. "I'm sorry. But it isn't my fault."

"Is there no way I can stay?" Cathy's voice sounded weak.

The woman shook her head so hard, her chins wobbled. "Nah. I've promised him that room ages ago."

She pursed her lips. "It's easy to find something else." Then she continued hauling herself up the steps.

The conversation was over.

Cathy schlepped herself down the steps and left the house. She barely noticed the steep angle of the street, nor the smell of the Chinese take-away at the corner. When a bus came roaring up the street within one inch of her, she didn't blink. Someone pushed her on the side-walk. She didn't react. Homeless. She was homeless.

When she reached the park, she let loose, her feet hammering the ground. She knew that was no way to build up her stamina, but tonight, she didn't care. She just wanted to get it out of her system.

Get rid of the fear, of the desperation that seized her.

Something wet ran down her cheeks and and blurred her vision. Tears? She'd never felt them coming. With a jerk, she tried to wipe them away. All of a sudden, she lost her footing at the edge of the way. Her right foot slipped and came down at an impossible angle. Some-thing tore inside. Pain shot through her ankle like liquid fire. Cathy fell down and hit her elbow hard on the ground. She cried out loud. Instinctively, she covered her ankle with both hands, as if that could make the pain go away.

She tried to get back in control. For an instant, she heard nothing but her blood pounding in her ears and felt the pain pulsating through her ankle. But it didn't get better, instead, the pain seemed to increase. Cathy started to cry without restraint. Her sobs came from deep within her and made her whole body jerk. Tears splashed down on her shorts and left dark blotches on the soft material.

"You all right, ma'am?"

Two boys stopped next to her. Cathy tried to wipe away the tears. "I . . . I think I've sprained my ankle." Her voice was shaking.

The boys glanced at each other, clearly with no idea what to do. Cathy tried to get a grip on herself, tried to concentrate on them. All arms and legs, she judged them to be fourteen, maybe a little bit older.

"If you helped me up, I might manage to walk home," she said. "Maybe you could assist me in taking off my shoe first?"

"Sure." They were willing, but rather clumsy about it. Cathy clenched her teeth. It felt as if they were sawing her foot off. Little stars shot through her vision. She closed her eyes and willed them to go away.

"Ma'am?"

Cathy opened her eyes and forced herself to smile. The boys obviously expected her to drop dead any moment. "Thank you." She held out her hand. "Let's try to get me up, all right?" The boys nodded. They were just a little bit taller than she was, but with their combined help, she managed to stand up straight, wobbling a little on one leg, like a flamingo. Swallowing hard, she tried to put her injured foot to the ground. Impossible. The slightest movement made pain lick up inside. With a rueful smile, she seized up the boys. "Do you think you could support me as far as the exit?"

They both nodded. Sweet kids. Cathy put her arms around their slim shoulders and tried one hop. The movement shook her ankle and reverberated inside her. Cathy pressed her lips together. Another hop. And yet another.

The boys giggled. She couldn't blame them, it probably looked most amusing. If only it didn't hurt so much.

By the time they had reached the exit, she was out of breath and close to tears again. "Thanks," she said. "You were great."

"There's a doc just down the block," one of the boys said as if it were a dubious thing to know. "We could bring you there."

Cathy had planned on getting a taxi, but his idea was better. She wouldn't have relished explaining to the driver her money was at home. "That would be wonderful."

It was the longest block she'd ever seen. Her good leg trembled with sheer exhaustion by the time they reached the door of the practice.

When a white-clad nurse came out and took over, her tears started to flow again. She barely managed to say good-bye to the boys who made their escape at high speed.

Sniffing into a tissue the nurse had provided, she answered all her questions in a low voice. Her name. Where she lived. The name of her insurance company. If she ever had trouble with that foot before.

At long last, the nurse got up. "The doctor will see you soon." Glancing at Cathy, she hesitated, then said,

"You're badly shaken. Do you wish me to call somebody to come and pick you up?"

Cathy's tears started to flow again. She could call Mick. Surely he would come. He would take her to his little house with the garden full of grass and roses, and he would look after her, caring for her. . . . "No," she said. "There's no one."

The nurse looked at her a little longer, then nodded. "We'll call a taxi when you're finished. You don't live far away."

Twenty minutes later, the doctor eased her foot in different directions. Cathy watched his movements with clenched teeth. She didn't like him. He was a bully.

"You're lucky." The doctor rolled her foot in his hand as if it were a joystick. "It's just a sprained ankle. The nurse will bandage it to give it some hold. We'll also give you a crutch, but you should rest your foot for the next three days."

Cathy stared at him. "What do you mean?"

The doctor lifted his eyebrows. His light eyes pierced her. "I mean you should avoid moving. Put your foot up. Rest." He talked as if she were an idiot.

"For three whole days?"

"At least. Is that a problem?"

"Of course it is a problem." Cathy frowned. "I've got to go to work."

The doctor seemed to be used to dealing with irritated people. "What kind of work do you do?"

"I work in an office."

He nodded. "Good. Let's see . . . Today's Wednesday.

I advise you not to go to work the next two days. Then you'll have the weekend on top of that. On Friday, you should come to see me again. It might be possible to return to the office on Monday, but make sure you put your foot up whenever you can."

Cathy swallowed. It was one thing to start a new life in a new city, quite another to be ill in one. She needed to find a room! How on earth was she going to manage?

The doctor gave her another piercing glance, then added, not unkindly, "You only have one body, you know. If you're sensible now, it'll soon be over. If not . . ." He let the unfinished sentence hang in air.

Cathy sighed. "Okay, I got the message." She pulled herself together. "Thank you."

The doctor smiled. "You're not good at accepting terms that are being dictated to you, are you?"

Cathy's mouth dropped open. She felt a smile spreading all over her face. "No. But I've just learned that."

The doctor grinned. "You'd have fooled me."

He was really a very sympathetic man.

The next morning, she called David and explained the situation.

"Of course you'd better rest," he said. "Take it easy."

Cathy was relieved. "I'm so sorry."

"That's no problem. By the way, Burlington-Brown called yesterday afternoon and told me he's very taken with you."

"He is?"

"Yeah. Well done, Cathy."

Cathy grinned. "He's an original."

David chuckled. "He sure is. But I knew you would handle him."

Cathy was glad he couldn't see her blushing. "Thank you."

"Well, take care, and I'll see you on Monday then. Bye."

"Bye."

Cathy nestled the phone into her bed cover as if it were precious. Her foot was swollen and hot, hurting a lot worse this morning, but her spirits soared. She was so glad David was happy with her.

Then she sighed. If only she knew how much that was going to count once she told him she was not going to marry Mick. She shook her head to clear her thoughts and decided she had to block out any thought of Mick. Of finding a room. Of her precarious position at work. She had to get well. One thing after the other, right?

What on earth was she going to think about? She'd never taken a Valium in her life. Maybe it was time to start now.

Chapter Thirteen

In the early afternoon, she grew so restless, she couldn't sit still. The TV offered nothing she could stomach, and talking of her stomach, it had started to make rumbling noises. She had finished every single orange, which happened so seldom, it made her feel as if she were left high and dry on an island.

She would have to order a pizza, only she was rather short on cash. Would they accept a credit card?

She'd spent the morning sleeping and painting her toenails dark red. It looked cocky, the way they gleamed next to the white bandage on her ankle, and it made her feel better. Not much, but it was a start.

She contemplated them, wriggling them a little, and wondered with increasing concern what to do about her stomach, when there was a knock on the door.

Cathy jumped. Who could want her? "Come in!"

The door flew open and Angie rushed into the room, a dark blue scarf with silver threads flying behind her.

"Cathy! Gosh, that foot really looks bad! Does it hurt very much?"

Cathy grinned. She felt much better. "No, no, it's fine as long as I don't move. How come you're here?"

Angie picked up the only chair in the room, turned it with the back to the bed and dropped into it. She crossed her arms on its back and frowned at Cathy. "Dave called me about some tickets for a concert he had to cancel tonight. He mentioned Mick would probably not want them as he had to stay home and nurse your foot."

Cathy stared into her lap and swallowed. "Oh."

"Oh, precisely!" Angie said. "I know for a fact that Mick is out of town until tomorrow night, and I didn't know myself you're in Seattle!"

Cathy's head came up. "Did you tell Dave?"

Angie shook her head so hard, her hair flew around her face. "Nah. Who do you take me for? Dave mentioned you share an office with Harry."

She put her head to one side and slipped her scarf through her fingers. "I knew Harry pretty well some time ago. So I called him immediately and asked him if he knew where you lived and of course, he did."

"Oh?" Cathy's voice went up.

Angie narrowed her eyes. "Your tongue isn't hurt, is it?"

Cathy had to laugh. "I just wondered how he knew. I never gave him my address."

Angie shook her head again. "He's like that. He knows where every good-looking woman lives."

Cathy grinned.

Angie moved her hand as if she wanted to wipe something away. "But I didn't come to talk about Harry. I want to know about you and Mick."

Cathy averted her face. "There's nothing to know."

"But surely . . ."

"Angie, do you have cash?"

Angie blinked.

"I'm starving, but I only have two dollars twenty left in my purse, and that's not going to buy us a pizza."

Angie threw back her head and laughed. "Between your riches and mine, we should manage something."

While choosing from the menu and directing Angie to find plates and silverware, Cathy managed to stall her another twenty minutes. Then the pizza came, and as soon as they settled down to eat, Angie got back on track.

"What went wrong between you and Mick?"

"What should have gone wrong?" Cathy struggled to sound casual, but there was a flutter in her stomach. She crammed a piece of her tuna pizza into her mouth.

"Well, one day you're as good as engaged, the next you're not talking anymore."

"We were never engaged." Cathy sat up straight. "Remember, we just staged the whole thing."

Angie rolled her eyes and stabbed at a piece of her Quattro Stagioni Pizza. "Don't give me that crap. It may have started like that, but in the end, you didn't have to fake anything anymore."

Cathy's throat constricted. She didn't know what to say. The piece of pizza in her mouth tasted like sawdust.

"Why did you walk out on him?" Angie asked.

"I didn't walk out on him!" Cathy's plate started to slide from her outstretched legs. She shot forward and grabbed it before it fell to the floor.

Angie put a piece of salami into her mouth and shrugged. "Well, that's what Mick said."

"What?" Cathy didn't believe her ears. "I never walked out on him!"

"What did you do, then?"

Cathy stared at her. "Why, nothing. I . . . I had to go back to Spokane with Dan. I . . . I mean, I couldn't just stay. I had a job." All of a sudden, it sounded feeble, even to her own ears. It wasn't the whole story, of course. But Angie would never understand.

Angie continued eating as if they were discussing different ways to clean a telephone. "Didn't sound like that when Mick told me about it."

"He never called me, the whole time I was in Spokane!" Cathy almost shouted at her.

Angie looked up, straight into her eyes. "Well, if you told someone you loved him, and he turned around and left without a word and then never called or gave a sign, would you think he wanted to be in touch?"

Cathy's heart missed a beat. "Is that what Mick said?"

Angie finished her pizza. "Yep."

Cathy lost her grip on the plate. "But . . . but I never meant . . ."

Angie shook her head. "At least he doesn't know yet you're here, so you can still save the day."

Cathy stared at her. "But he does."

"He does?"

Cathy nodded.

"So you finally called him? Well done!"

"Er, no." Cathy swallowed. "I met him by chance at a business meeting. Yesterday."

Angie's mouth dropped open. "No way."

"Yes. But when I asked him to join me for a cup of coffee, he refused!"

"Don't tell me that surprised you."

Cathy jumped. "Of course it did! I mean, if he cared for me, he wouldn't have refused, would he?"

"Oh no?" Angie put her hands on her hips. "No? You must be very sure of yourself!"

Cathy blinked. "What do you mean? I'm not!"

Angie frowned. "Well, suppose you tell a guy you love him. He turns around and leaves without a word. That's pretty explicit, I would say. Next, you meet him by chance some weeks later, and he actually lives in town and has never tried to be in touch."

Cathy stared at her, her mouth dry.

Angie continued. "Would you believe this person is interested in you?"

Cathy's hand crept to her mouth. "But I . . ." She couldn't finish her sentence. Her plate crashed to the ground and cracked into pieces. Cathy didn't move.

"But perhaps you really don't care for Mick? I'd

have sworn the thing between you two was genuine, but maybe here I am, pestering you, and all the time you're glad you got rid of him?"

"No!" Cathy almost jumped out of her bed in spite of her protesting ankle. "I . . . I do care." She'd never admitted it aloud. So she had hurt Mick? She'd never wanted that. Not for the world. "Angie . . ." She swallowed. "I was a fool."

Angie bent down to retrieve the pizza. "Glad you say so."

Cathy gripped Angie's wrist. "Tell me."

"What?" Angie straightened.

"Does he . . . does Mick really care?"

Angie shrugged. "I'm not a shrink. But he carries that picture of Frances' birthday party around in his wallet and gets real angry if somebody happens to see it."

"Oh."

"Also, he avoids Frances. And me. And David. Everyone who met you. When I asked a perfectly innocent question about you, he bit my head off."

Cathy closed her eyes for a second.

"He works like crazy. But he doesn't talk about it the way he used to." Angie narrowed her eyes. "You know, he always tried to explain some stupid sort of grass or other to me. I'd never have thought I'd miss it one day." She stared at the broken plate and pizza on the ground and added, "I'll clean up this mess. You'd better get well soon. And then do something about it."

She knelt down and picked up a piece of Cathy's plate. "I just hope it's not too late."

Something constricted in Cathy's chest. "Why?"

"That nasty bit of work Nicole is hanging around him all the time."

On Friday evening, Cathy returned to the doctor once more. "Please make the bandage as tight as possible. I have to go out tomorrow."

His blue eyes pierced her as before. "It's a matter of life and death?" His voice was ironic.

Cathy pressed her lips together. "It is."

When she dropped into her bed that night, she couldn't fall asleep. Maybe Mick wasn't in town. But no, Angie had told her he had planned to return home tonight. Of course she could call him and make a date. But what if he said no? She couldn't explain on the phone. No, there was just one thing to do. She had to go to his house and face him, to tell him how sorry she was.

Tossing and turning, she tried to decide what time would be best to surprise a man on a Saturday morning.

9:00 A.M.? Surely that was too early.

10:00 A.M.? Might be good. Unless he'd gone to bed late the night before. How she wished she knew him better. Was he an early riser? What if she woke him? Surely he wouldn't like to be woken up by an earnest woman, bent on declaring her love. How embarrassing.

Maybe 11:00 A.M. was better. But no, he would long be gone by then. Shopping. Or maybe he took out his boat for a trip across the Sound.

It was all very difficult.

With a sigh, she sat up. She needed to brush her teeth again. It would soothe her and make her feel better. Cathy got out of bed by moving her foot an inch at a time to avoid jarring it. She angled for her crutches and hopped into the bathroom. In the mirror, her eyes looked tiny and red, her hair like the nest of a chaotic bird. She blinked, looked away, and started to brush her teeth with fierce determination.

It was easier for men. They bought a bunch of red roses and that was it.

Easy.

The language of flowers, no more need for words. But she couldn't bring herself to buy a big bunch of red roses. She'd look completely ridiculous, wouldn't she? Of course she tried to be an emancipated woman. But buying roses for a man was beyond her limit. She'd feel so peculiar. Cathy frowned, spat the foam into the sink, and rinsed her mouth.

Then, out of the blue, a thought came to her. She brought herself up with a jerk. She would buy him something, to have it in her hands if words failed her altogether. She'd buy him a plant. A grass, to be exact. Yes, that was a good idea.

They could talk about the grass first. Then she wouldn't have to come right out. She had worried all day how to start the conversation. Simply by saying "I love you"? That was rather rushing the fences. Maybe it would be better to explain first. Why she had acted the way she had. But would he listen long enough? It was all so complicated.

She hopped out of the bathroom and switched on her computer. She'd Google it. Nurseries in Seattle. She had to find one, preferably on her way to his house since she had to take a taxi because of her foot.

The Internet listed more nurseries than she had expected. But for some reason, not a single one talked about grasses specifically. Cathy rubbed her left shoulder. They probably belonged to some group. What on earth were perennials anyway? She would have to take potluck. Finally, she chose a large retail nursery in Crown Hill and noted the address on a yellow Post-it that she stuck on her mirror.

When she returned to her bed, she hesitated. Was it a ridiculous idea altogether? Maybe he would laugh in her face . . . or throw the grass at her . . . or give it to Nicole. She swallowed and decided to try to sleep before she could envision more nightmares. Tomorrow . . . tomorrow would be a turning point in her life. She was so afraid.

Chapter Fourteen

"I'd like to buy a grass, please." Cathy tried to speak as if it wasn't the most important purchase she'd ever made.

The woman in front of her had short, iron gray hair that showed she didn't like to spend hours in front of the mirror. Her smile revealed a multitude of wrinkles in her sunburned face. "Sure. What kind of grass?"

Cathy recoiled. "I . . . I'm not sure. It should be special."

The woman put her head to one side. "We have five acres of display and quite a few specials among them, so I'm sure we can find something. Should the grass be large or small?"

"Oh." Cathy hadn't thought about it. "Well. So I can carry it."

Now the woman laughed outright. "I meant when it's

fully grown. Should it be large or small? Where do you plan to plant it?"

Cathy could feel her face reddening. This was almost as difficult as buying a car. "It's for a friend." She heard the desperation in her voice.

The woman smiled. "Maybe it's best if I show you what we have on display."

"Yes." Cathy nodded. "Yes, that sounds like a good idea."

The woman led her through a glass house that was so large it could shelter a train.

When they stepped out into the garden, a small sound of delight escaped Cathy's lips. It was like a huge park, with narrow alleys leading through it. To her right and left, colors exploded from a million buds. Tiny blue ones, formed like stars, filled a whole shelf. ASTER. Cathy could read the first word of a complicated name on a sign before she hurried past them on her crutches.

They passed another ocean of buds that smelled tartly. This time, the buds were filled with leaves as if someone had crammed twice as many as planned into the blossom. They frilled in ever decreasing circles toward a center that could only be guessed at, well protected deep inside. The colors ranged from orange to bronze to dark red, intense and pure.

"How beautiful." Cathy had never seen such a large nursery before. Mick would know it. He may even visit it quite often. What a nice job he had.

"There you are." The sales woman indicated the area in front of her with a wide sweep of her hand.

Cathy stared. To her right-hand side reigned a grass, planted in a plastic container that almost reached up to her knees. Long, feathery plumes shot out of the center, as if they wanted to pierce the sky like silver arrows. They were surrounded by a swinging court of long, thin blades. A breeze caressed them and made them rustle like lovers whispering to each other.

"It's lovely, isn't it?" The woman smiled at her. "It's the right season to buy grass; most of it looks best right now."

Cathy nodded, unable to wrench her gaze away. If she could offer him that! But it was unthinkable; she couldn't even move it an inch, let alone carry it. "What is it?"

"*Cortaderia selloana.*"

"Ah."

The woman smiled. "It's also called Pampas grass."

"Do you have something like that, only smaller?" Cathy looked around.

The woman frowned. "Weeell . . . there's a grass I love. It doesn't get very high though; at the most, it'll reach up to your knees."

"That wouldn't matter."

"The botanical name for it is *Stipa tenuissima*, but it's dubbed Angel Hair."

Cathy smiled. "That sounds nice."

"Yes." The woman bent down and retrieved a small container that contained a shaggy wisp of grass. "This is it."

In dismay, Cathy stared at the container that showed

more black brown earth than anything else. The weak grass struggled like a piece of weed right in the middle. "This is it? But that's . . ." She broke off. "I'm sorry, but I can't offer it as a gift."

"Oh." The saleswoman glanced at the plant, then back at Cathy. There was a twinkle in her eyes. "I see what you mean." She put the container down. "I believe we have larger ones over here." She searched a bit down the path, then retrieved another, much larger container that she had to grip with both hands. "Is that more like it?"

The grass was a bunch of hundreds of finest blades, light green at the bottom, then feathering out into larger heads with a pale golden hue. As it moved in her hands, the sun came out from behind a wall of clouds and touched it. Immediately, the grass seemed to be filled with life, a thousand shimmering blond tops, tousled by the breeze.

Cathy cleared her throat. "I can see how it got its name."

"Yes, it's wonderful, isn't it?"

Cathy glanced back at the miniature container they had put back. "And the other one will look the same?"

The woman nodded. "Sure. Next year or the year afterward, at the latest."

"Incredible."

"It needs to have sandy soil," the woman said as they walked back along the aisle. She carried the grass for Cathy. "Wet feet aren't good for it."

"Okay." Cathy hopped behind her and wondered

what kind of soil Mick's garden had. With her usual luck, it was going to be marsh land.

She asked the taxi driver to place the grass next to Mick's front door, then paid him with shaking hands. Mick's car stood in the drive. He had to be at home.

When she turned back to the door she'd seen so often in her dreams, she took a deep breath and struggled to steady herself. It didn't help. Her heart was drumming so loud, she couldn't hear another sound. She stopped breathing altogether when she rang his bell.

Nothing.

Cathy checked her watch for the hundredth time. A quarter past ten.

Was he still asleep? She didn't want to wake him.

She waited long enough for him to wake up, get oriented, brush his teeth, and go to the door.

Then she rang again. The sound of the bell reverberated inside the small house, but she could hear nothing else.

Cathy stood stiff, listening hard. Was there a movement behind the door? A bird chirped somewhere, but the sound only emphasized the silence inside.

Cathy sagged against the door. He wasn't home. Maybe Nicole had picked him up. Her disappointment hit her so hard, she almost cried.

She would have to wait. There was no sense in going back, after having geared herself up to face it.

What if he decided to stay out of town for one more day? You'll wait until you're covered by moss.

She tried to ignore the nasty voice inside and hopped around the corner onto the porch. The Adirondack chairs faced the sea, just as she remembered them. It seemed like a foreign place without Mick. She felt like an intruder.

She stopped in front of the chairs and eyed them with misgiving. They were not made for people who had a hard time to get up again.

Then she remembered her grass. He shouldn't see it before he saw her. She limped back. It was heavier than she had imagined. Shoving and pulling it, always trying not to put any weight on her foot, she managed to push it alongside the first Adirondack chair. Out of breath, she stopped.

Right.

She might as well sit down now. She could be here for some time.

With a sigh, she collapsed into the chair and placed her crutch beside her. The wooden armrest felt soft beneath her fingers. She followed the structure of the wood with her fingertips, then looked around.

A few late roses were still blooming at the railing, but it was obvious autumn wasn't far away. Some leaves had turned yellow, and she could spot a few rose hips. They had a funny shape, like a large drop of water. Trust Mick to find a special rose for his home. For no reason at all, her throat constricted with a rush of tenderness.

She tore her eyes away, to the garden. So many kinds of grasses, different colors, different heights. As she watched, a slight breeze blew across them and bowed the heads as if an invisible hand caressed them from above. Yes, this was high season for grasses. As far as she could tell, there was no Angel Hair among it. Probably because it was marshland.

At the horizon, lofty clouds sailed over the deep blue sky. When she had set out, they'd formed a massive wall, but now, it had broken up, and the sun highlighted the garden for minutes on end. The change between shadow and light played on the shrubs and gave the whole garden an evasive and unreal air.

Cathy inhaled the salty smell of the sea.

It was so beautiful and peaceful. Paradise. Without Adam, though.

Suddenly, a car roared up the drive.

It had to be Mick.

Her mouth went dry.

The car stopped in front of the house, a door banged. She heard steps coming closer.

With hammering heart, Cathy struggled out of her seat. She couldn't remember a single word to say.

In slow motion, she turned to the corner. He would enter the house, never dreaming she was here. She had to go and meet him at the door. But her feet didn't obey.

All at once, a doorbell tore through the silence. Cathy froze.

It couldn't be Mick.

The postman, maybe?

She staggered back to her chair and dropped into it.

The visitor rushed around the corner and stopped right in front of her. "What are you doing here?"

Nicole. Looking more than ever like a supermodel, with white slacks, elegant sandals, and a tailored top.

Cathy immediately felt dowdy.

She smiled, more out of habit than anything. "Hi."

Without thinking, she inched closer to her grass and tried to cover it with her skirt. Which was stupid, after all it was a rather tight skirt. But somehow, she couldn't bear for Nicole to see her gift. At least she hadn't chosen red roses.

Of course her move of protection didn't help. On the contrary, Nicole's eyes fixed on the grass. Cathy had asked for gift packaging to hide the plastic container, so it stood there in all its splendor of yellow tissue paper with dark green ribbons. At the shop, she'd thought it decorative because it emphasized the colors of the grass. Now it seemed showy.

Nicole threw back her head and laughed. "You've bought a grass for Mick?" Laughter came out of her perfect mouth in gasps, until she had to hold herself by the railing to avoid falling. "That's like offering bread to a baker!"

Cathy felt like crying. Of course. It had seemed like such a good idea, but now she could see it had been stupid. Fighting hard to keep her feelings from her face, she failed to answer. Not a single witty thing came to her mind.

Nicole finally stopped laughing and wiped her eyes. Which was for show, there was not a single drop of tears on those extraordinary triangular lashes.

All of a sudden, Cathy hated her.

"You shouldn't hang around and wait for him." Nicole leaned against the porch railing, completely at ease. She crossed her elegant ankles, then checked the expensive watch on her slim wrist. "Mick will be here any minute, but he promised to take me out for lunch, so it's a waste of time, really."

Oh no. Please, it can't be true. She'd never even thought of that. Cathy couldn't move.

Nicole put her head to one side. Her black hair cascaded down her shoulder like a shimmering waterfall. "Have you lost your voice or something?"

Cathy pulled herself together. "No."

Nicole smiled. The smile did not improve her charm. In fact, it was chilling. "You know, you look as if you're waiting for a bus."

Cathy sat there, frozen, awkward and hated herself, hated Nicole. If only she looked like Nicole. If only she had an answer to all those stabs.

Nicole dropped into the chair next to Cathy. "I like your skirt." She gave Cathy a conspiratorial smile, from woman to woman. "I had a similar one a few years ago."

Cathy would have run at that moment. But to struggle up out of her deep chair, clumsy like an albatross, being watched by that exquisite woman, kept her glued down.

She stared at her feet. Her ankle had started to throb again and hurt like a demon from within. The red nail polish on her toes was the wrong color, she could see that now. She'd been so proud of them. She tried to hide her feet beneath the chair.

"Cathy!" Mick stood on the porch.

She'd never heard him coming.

His lips were pale.

Before Cathy could open her mouth, Nicole jumped up, flung herself at Mick, and hugged him. Cathy felt a stab. They made a splendid couple . . . as if they were posing for a magazine or something.

But suddenly, she saw it. Mick held Nicole as if he didn't want to, his arms barely curved, his back straight. He stared over Nicole's shoulder at Cathy. His lion eyes held a puzzled expression.

Cathy had no idea what he saw in her face, but he put Nicole to the side much as one moves a piece of furniture. Three long strides brought him up short in front of her chair. "What happened to your foot?"

Cathy's mouth felt dry. "Sprained ankle." Her heart was beating so hard, it seemed to explode in her chest. She was aware of Nicole standing behind him, a frown on her perfect face.

"Does it hurt very much?" he asked. It sounded stilted, as if he wasn't quite himself either.

She didn't feel her ankle at all. "No."

Nicole placed a hand on Mick's shoulder. "Mick, we'd better go. You were late already and I—"

"I can't come with you." Mick didn't take his eyes off Cathy.

Nicole recoiled. "What?"

Mick lifted his eyebrows. "I can't leave Cathy on the doorstep now, can I?"

Cathy was glad Nicole did not carry a knife or she would have been afraid for her life.

"We could take her with us and drop her on the way," Nicole said.

Push me out of the car, you mean. Cathy cleared her throat. "In fact . . ."

"She wanted to bring you that grass." Nicole made a move with her shapely head in the rough direction of the grass. "Now that it's done, we can take her home. She didn't bring a car."

Mick swung around and stared at the grass. Cathy clenched her hands in her lap. If only Nicole weren't here.

"*Stipa tenuissima?*" He smiled. "How nice." His eyes met Cathy's. The puzzled expression was still there, but underneath, she could see something else. A warmth that made her giddy.

"Mick, we really have to be going." Nicole almost danced with impatience.

"I'm not coming, Nicole." His tone was final.

"But you promised we would talk about the last changes to the garden today!" She looked magnificent in her rage, with flashing dark eyes.

He nodded. "I know I did. I'm sorry, but I can't make it. Can I call you later today to arrange another time?"

She narrowed her eyes. "So that's it? Private things are more important than your business? I'll make sure to pass on that information, Mick Vandenholt."

Cathy caught her breath. It was a business date only? The way Nicole had phrased it earlier, she had been sure they had arranged a private lunch. Suddenly, it struck her that it was barely eleven o'clock. Much too early for lunch.

Mick sighed. "Nicole, I have been at your beck and call for weeks now. Don't you think it's acceptable to postpone our meeting just once?"

Nicole jutted her chin. It sat strangely on her, like a pair of glasses on a fairy tale princess. "I tell you, I'm not going to accept it, and I will talk about it. You will notice."

Cathy sat at the edge of her chair.

Mick shrugged. "By all means. But you shouldn't forget it may be viewed as the exaggeration of a jealous woman."

Cathy's mouth dropped open.

"Me? Jealous?" Nicole glanced at Cathy with contempt. "Of that sparrow?"

Mick grinned. "A sparrow?" He looked at Cathy's red shirt. "More like a robin today, isn't she?"

Without another word, Nicole flung herself off the porch. The heels of her sandals clattered around the corner. They heard the door of her car bang. Almost simultaneously, the motor started. With shrieking wheels, the car sped away.

It was quiet on the porch. The scent of warm wood drifted up from the floor boards, gone in a second. Mick crossed his arms and leaned against the railing. His eyes probed Cathy's face.

Cathy was unable to say a word. She attempted to

find again the trace of warmth that would give her the courage to start, but it was gone. Darn Nicole.

"Why did you come?" The tone was friendly, but his face remained blank.

All of a sudden, she knew she had to stand. She couldn't remain seated, her head thrown back as far as it would go to see him properly.

She gripped the broad armrests of her chair and pushed herself up. Mick bent forward and supported her at the elbow. For a fleeting moment, she was close enough to smell his skin. Her knees buckled under, but she managed to pretend she had lost her balance.

She leaned sideways against the railing and faced him, gripping the top slat with her right hand.

His hand dropped as soon as she stood safely, leaving her all alone.

Cathy took a deep breath. "I came to apologize."

Inside the house, his telephone started to ring.

Cathy closed her eyes. It couldn't be true. He would go and answer it. She would return to her chair and fall asleep. Then it would go on and on, forever and ever, and she would never, ever manage to tell him what she was struggling to say.

"Go on."

The telephone rang louder now, demanding attention.

She made a weak movement with her hand. "But the phone . . ."

"I'm not going to be interrupted by that darn phone another time," he said. "Let it ring."

When she didn't manage to reply, he said, "You came to apologize, you said. What for?"

Cathy stared into the garden. At the foot of the porch, tiny white flowers nestled into cushions of silvery leaves. Green and white, they foamed against the wood like the crest of a wave. Cathy gathered all the courage she had. "That morning after Frances' birthday, you said . . ." Cathy stopped, not knowing how to express it.

". . . About me. Us. You said . . ." Her voice trailed off.

His eyes intent, he nodded. "I know what I said."

Cathy breathed a sigh of relief. "Yes. Then . . . then Dan called. Somehow, he rushed me back to Spokane."

She met his lion eyes, then quickly corrected herself. "I let myself be rushed away." Somehow, it sounded like a distorted sentence, but Mick seemed to understand. He nodded again, not interrupting her. He wasn't standing close to her, but her body was fully conscious of his.

"When . . . when I was back in Spokane, I wanted to call you. A million times."

"You didn't." His voice was flat.

"No." She rushed on, eager to make him understand. "You see, I . . . I knew if I contacted you, I wouldn't be able to resist you."

He moved then. As quick as lightning, he stepped closer, but stopped just before touching her. "Yes?"

"I'm not sure if you'll understand. I told you I started the whole thing because I needed to be more independent." She searched his face. "You know, all of my life

Dan managed everything. I mean everything. I never even paid an electricity bill on my own. It has been ages since I wrote a check by myself; I barely know how anymore. You see?"

Mick nodded.

It got easier now. "So I decided to move out, to learn to be on my own. Try my wings." She smiled a little. "I had barely started when I hit your van. The next thing I knew, I was head over heels in love with you."

She heard his sharp intake of breath, but his tone was dry. "I'd never have guessed."

Her smile deepened. "Only because I got away as soon as I could. You read me like a book."

He pushed back his hair in a gesture so familiar she felt her chest tighten with tenderness. Before she could get stuck again, she continued. "When Dave called and offered me that job, I was so happy. I'd made it, all on my own. Later, I had my doubts. After all, you might have instigated the whole thing."

"I didn't."

"No. I know that now."

"Why didn't you contact me when you came to Seattle?" he asked.

She averted her face. "Dan said . . ."

He sighed. "What did Dan have to say this time?"

She pressed her lips together. "He said I was just changing my protector, so to speak."

"Kind words."

"Yeah. But maybe true."

"Would it have been true?" he asked.

"No." She lifted her hands, then dropped them again. "Yes." She shook her head. "Oh, I don't know. It's not the same at the roots, but in the end, it may have the same effect." She bit her lips.

"I'm not Dan," Mick said.

"But you're a man."

Finally, he smiled. She saw his dimple emerge in his cheek. "I hope that's not a problem."

She had to chuckle. "Well, no. I don't think so. But you see why I couldn't contact you, don't you?"

Slowly, he nodded. "Yes."

For a minute, neither said a word. Then he asked, an odd smile hovering at the corners of his mouth, "Is that all?" His voice was tender.

Cathy gasped. "Isn't that enough?"

"I feared a lot worse." He touched her cheek, soft as a butterfly. "But you of all people should know I understand the need for freedom."

Cathy wanted to believe him, but she didn't dare to. "Do you think so?"

He pulled her close to him. "I do." For an instant, his lion eyes smiled into hers, then he bent his head and kissed her.

A breeze rustled the grass in the garden and somewhere, out on the blue edge of the ocean, a seagull shrieked. Cathy flew high like a swallow, arching in the blue sky, overwhelmed by pure happiness—until Angie's voice came from directly behind her. "Is that the rehearsal for the breakup?"

Cathy felt a wave of heat going to her head and would have broken away if Mick had not put his arm around her shoulder and kept her close.

"Because if it is . . ." Angie grinned, ". . . it doesn't look very efficient to me."

"Go away." Mick sighed. "Go away and don't return until tomorrow. And make sure you tell everybody else to stay away too."

Cathy giggled. She couldn't suppress it, it came from deep inside her, her happiness bubbling over. Mick smiled at her, his dimple deepening.

Angie glanced from one to the other. "I'm not wanted." She grinned. "And I know it. I'll leave in a minute, but Mick, when I looked for you in the house just a minute ago, the phone rang, and I happened to hear the message that was left on your answering machine."

The phone? Cathy hadn't heard anything. But maybe that shouldn't surprise her.

Mick sighed. "It's a miracle you didn't pick it up."

Angie grinned at him. "As if I would do that! It was that guy from Chicago, the one who organized the Garden of Eden Contest. He said you got the bid!"

Cathy felt Mick stiffen. His head was bent down toward her, but she had the impression he didn't see her. Then he let go of her and wheeled around to stare across the garden.

"Oh." His voice was flat.

Angie opened her eyes wide. "Is that all you have to say? It's fabulous!"

"Yeah." Mick sounded as if they were discussing

cold coffee. "It's a compliment. But I'll decline it." He looked down at Cathy. "He's the guy who called the night of Frances' birthday. He'd gotten the time zones mixed up, as usual. Let's go inside."

He turned to go, but Cathy put her hand on his arm and held him back. She frowned. "Was it an important contest?"

"Important!" Angie threw up her hands. "It's one of the most prestigious bids he ever applied for. To think you got it and want to decline it! Have you gone mad, Mick?"

"Angela." Mick didn't raise his voice. "Will you for once shut up?"

Angie stamped her foot. "No, I won't! You told me it was your dream to get it, and now you're telling me you won't accept it! What on earth has gotten into you?"

Cathy smiled at her and said, "Angie, please leave us alone for a minute, will you?"

Angie pursed her lips.

"Please."

"Oh, all right." Angie pivoted around. "Since you are going to be my sister-in-law someday, I guess I'd better get on your good side."

"Well done." Mick sounded surprised. "I was never able to get rid of her."

"I'm getting a lot of practice." Cathy smiled. "I even drove someone away I'd rather keep close."

She saw the smile back in his eyes, the smile that was the reason she had fallen for him in the first place. "Is that so?" He pulled her close.

"Wait a minute." Cathy put her hands on his chest to hold him off.

He loosened his hold immediately.

"Why do you plan to refuse the bid?"

He just looked at her.

"Remember our promise?" Cathy smiled at him. It was delicious to be so close to him. "We said we would be honest."

"Oh well." He pushed back his hair. "I . . . it would involve working in Chicago for half a year."

Cathy tried to read his face. "Yes?"

"Isn't it obvious? I don't want to be away from you for such a long time."

Her heart did some kind of somersault in her chest.

He pulled her closer. "Do you know that these last weeks, whenever I closed my eyes, all I could see was your face, your eyes, looking at me the way you look right now? I tried to make it go away, but I couldn't."

Cathy put her arms around his neck. "Mick?"

"Hmmm?"

"You should accept."

There was a pause, then he asked, "Why?"

She leaned back in his arms, to see his face better. "Because you would always be sorry later. Half a year is not very much compared to . . . compared to a lifetime. It's dangerous to sacrifice a dream. It might come back when you're tired, and you might regret it." She hesitated, but went on to say it anyway. "If . . . if our love is true, then it won't come to harm from six months." She took a deep breath. "Besides, it would give me time to learn to be on my own."

He lifted his eyebrows. "I thought you'd already learned that?"

She made a wry mouth. "Three weeks of independence? That's not a lot, is it? I haven't even found a place to live."

His eyes widened. "What do you mean? Where are you staying?"

"At a bed-and-breakfast on the edge of the International District. I've hunted for a room for ages, but they're all dreadful, and I feel like a total loser. You wouldn't believe the places I've seen, Mick. One had . . ."

He frowned. "There's something I don't understand." He held her away from him and searched her face.

"Yes?"

"Why did you come to my house today if you still feel the need to be on your own? It doesn't make sense."

She swallowed. "You're right. It doesn't." She hunted for the right words, but failed to find them. Her eyes dropped to his chest and fixed themselves on a button of his linen shirt. The mother-of-pearl glittered in the light. He smelled intoxicating. Of some good aftershave, of skin and . . . and just him.

"Cathy."

She lifted her head. "Yes?"

"Remember our promise?" A small smile sat in the corner of his mouth.

She had to laugh and lifted her hands in a gesture of

surrender. She would just speak her mind. He would understand. Her words poured out in a rush. "I came because Angie said I'd hurt you, and I couldn't bear that thought. I didn't want to hurt you. I just wanted to learn to make it on my own. But somehow, that wasn't possible without breaking so much. I hurt Dan, then I hurt you. And you . . . you had done nothing wrong. It wasn't fair. That's why I decided to come and explain it all."

His hands dropped from her shoulders. He drew back a pace. "So you still feel you should remain on your own, but out of compassion, you came?"

She jumped. Pain soared through her ankle, but she ignored it. "No! Oh no. I have accomplished something. I mean, a bit. Of course it's not enough yet, but . . ." She cut off in midsentence, then added, "You . . . you said you're not Dan."

He put his head to one side. "That sounds a little muddled."

She looked up at him. "That's probably because I am muddled."

His smile was tender. "Have you never considered there are all kinds of love? There are independent women who develop into mice when they get married. I don't see why it shouldn't work vice versa."

Cathy stared at him. "You mean . . . ?"

He put his hands on her shoulders again. "I mean it's up to us what we make of it." His lion eyes held hers. "I believe real love involves a lot of freedom. Freedom to be yourself." He frowned. "What have I said to make you cry?"

Cathy wiped her tears away and smiled. "Nothing. Everything. Oh Mick, I'm so glad I overlooked that stop sign."

"Mick, my ankle hurts. Can we sit down?"

"Sure." He watched her hopping to the Adirondack chair. "You know, you don't remind me of a robin, but a crow. They hop over the fields just like you."

"Hm. You're supposed to be in the first idiotic stages of love . . ."

"But I am." He held out his hand to her.

She took it. "Well, if that makes me a crow, what on earth will you compare me to when you've reached the sensible stage?"

"By then, you'll be an eagle, of course," he said without hesitation and pulled her with him into the chair. Settling her sideways, he lifted her leg and placed it on the broad armrest, so her ankle came to rest on the armrest of the second chair that stood alongside theirs. "A small eagle, though." He smiled. Then his lips came down over hers, and he kissed her in a way she'd never been kissed before.

Finally, Cathy eased back. She still had to get the last issue out of the way. If she wasn't going to do it now, she would never do it. "You know, I meant it when I said you should accept the Chicago offer."

He moved beneath her. "I hate the idea of going away. If I hadn't been so miserable, I would never have applied. Though of course it's a huge step forward in my career, I admit that."

He took her hands. "But even if I didn't count you . . . just the idea of leaving my house gives me the jitters. If I rented it out, someone is sure to come and . . ." He stopped and stared at his garden.

". . . chop all the heads off the grass blades?" Cathy grinned.

He laughed. "How on earth do you know about that?"

"Frances told me."

He sighed. "Of course. Yes, that's one thing I fear. Or worse." All of a sudden, he jerked. "I've got it! You'll move into my house. If you do that, I'll go to Chicago."

"Mick, I can't move into your house!" Cathy sat up straight.

"No?" he said, a smile deep in his eyes that made her catch her breath. "I'll even let you pay the electricity bill, if you want to. Or come to think of it, all the bills. Now ain't that generous?"

Her mouth twitched. "Very."

"No, but seriously. What is there to say against it?"

Cathy hesitated. "Nothing really. It's a dream. Only it seems to be so easy, and I wanted to prove to myself I can do it. Battle with landlords, all that stuff."

"There are plenty of battles waiting for you." Suddenly, he looked serious. "If you omit one, take it as a gift and don't feel any less independent for it."

She faltered. "Dan said . . ."

Mick sighed. "I knew we'd come back to Dan."

Cathy gripped his hands. "Mick, he predicted I would not manage to find a place, and that I would move in with you! He'll double over laughing with scorn."

"Clever move."

"What do you mean?"

"Well, he knew perfectly well you were going to do the opposite of what he said. So what's easier than to tell you to do something, to make sure you won't?"

Cathy caught her breath. "He wouldn't!"

Mick's eyebrows soared. "Oh no? Well, let me tell you, my girl, of course you are able to find a place all on your own. It's normal to see a million places you hate before you finally find the right one. That doesn't mean you're incapable. On the contrary."

Cathy rubbed her left shoulder. "You think so?"

His voice sounded more than ever like whiskey when he said, "I've missed that."

"What?"

"The way you rub your shoulder when you're mulling over something."

Cathy dropped her hand and stared at it. "Do I?"

He laughed. "All the time." He searched her face, and when she failed to answer, he asked, "Well?"

Cathy told herself she was a fool, but she had to say it. "I still don't think I can give up my fight for a room and feel I've made it."

His dimple appeared again. "I'll trade it against something equally horrible. Or worse."

"Like what?"

"Let me see. What's the worst thing an independent person has to do?"

He moved his hand through her hair, then opened the clasp that held it together. "You can't imagine how often I've dreamed of doing this."

Her pulse beat faster. "You're losing track."

"Yeah, I know." He took her face in both hands.

Cathy knew that in another second, she'd forget what they were discussing. So would he. "The worst thing?" she managed to say and leaned closer.

Mick drew a deep breath. "You can put together the annual files for the IRS. Clean the drain when it's blocked. Fill in forms for insurance companies. It's all yours. Did I tell you that I love you?"